73

UH-OH
THE COLLECTED POETRY, STORIES AND EROTIC SASS OF
DERRICK C. BROWN

☙

Edited by
Madison Mae Parker
and Sarah Johansson

Front Cover Design
Nik Ewing

Front Cover Photo
Matt Wignall

Front Cover Model
Amber Tamblyn

Write Bloody Publishing
America's Independent Press

Los Angeles, CA

1ˢᵗ edition.
ISBN: 978-1938912-62-7

Interior Layout by Madison Mae Parker
Cover Designed by Nik Ewing
Author Photo by Matt Wignall
Proofread by Sarah Johansson
Edited by Madison Mae Parker and Sarah Johansson
Type set in Bergamo from www.theleagueofmoveabletype.com

Printed in Tennessee, USA

Write Bloody Publishing
Los Angeles, CA
Support Independent Presses
writebloody.com

To contact the author, send an email to writebloody@gmail.com

MADE IN THE USA

UH-OH

UH-OH

All Energies of Death

Our Poison Horse

Strange Light

Scandalabra

I Love You is Back

Born in the Year of the Butterfly Knife

So now, you're a bit of gold to pound
back into the earth, the dew, of course,
forever lapping your toes,—
Frank, you dumb fuck,— who loves you
loves you regardless.

Thomas Lux

ALL ENERGIES OF DEATH

Every Coffin Is A Soap Box Derby

Tear apart every picture frame in the house and build that casket.
Wallpaper the roof of it with the photos
like your high school locker.
Load it with the images of all the animals and friends you loved.
Lie down in it with a new bullhorn,
letting them know that you blew it,
that what you 'knew' was wrong and it's fine,
that you should have planned less, undressed and just begun.
You should have been more strolling grateful
and less city of butt-rock and boring piss.
Holler gratefulness to the animals you killed
or that died around you, under your care, trying to make you see.
Lady and Sara, the dogs who hung on for you until you could
handle it.
Belteshazzar and Shazam, the doves you used in magic shows
who died in a cage of the flu because the way to stay warm
is flight.
Mr. Fish, who first met you when your huge white orb
landed in his bowl like a rescue buoy moon,
fine with the small world he ruled alone;
not the last thing to die of your boredom.
Mickey, the white mouse eaten by Minnie, the secret cannibal,
who got greedy and choked on her own tail. You dead bitch.
Ain't nothing Fine or Young about you.
Easter Bread, the wild rabbit living in your yard,
who you gave water to, who trusted you,
who grew tired of running from the neighbors' loose dogs
and gave in, proud of the races won.
Thank you for the master class.
You should've watched and learned
that language doesn't solve everything,
to fight at the right time, to surrender well,
to hold still and shake alone, clean your nasty out and eat it wild,
race down the grass on ice blocks and howl away nude in the night
realizing that untamed is the better solution.
Look at you. You're racing away. The lid is still open.
The details whiz by and you reach out to catch them,
but it's all flash paper.
You will gain speed and sing that the prize is wildness.
Chop up all them frames,

let yourself be scared as a pheasant realizing the decoy, too late,
too late. Pack the bags under your gaze.
Get into your solid black soap box derby for one.
Goodbye clean heroes. Goodbye marketable life. Goodbye
safe lethargy. Goodbye resurrected shame. Goodbye wallflower
botanist. Roll away proud. Sing out that you are not sorry. Forever
is for losers. You have got to go. Why not leave in a Champion face?
Cross the finish line and freeze in that Champion face. Goodbye.
You win. Close the lid.
It's getting warm. Look how the racer becomes a finish line.
Relax and give in to all the victoriously beautiful,
loving energies of death.

Ethernet Ballad
For Eugene and Katie

I first plugged her in.
Her report clearly states:

My Man.
My generous heart.
Champion of the odd.
Tear loofah.
I'm sorry the world doesn't want a TV show
called *Horseback Surprise*.
I do.
You solve my loneliness and lo-fi fear.
I'll make you a cocktail when you are down
with a jigger of cold beach
and a splash of helium
to lift your chin
when the forces of hmphf
are against you.

Shall I hide in the house before you get home
to scare the heavy day off of you?
I will. Your boo is meant to be scary.
Look at me and hear the jukebox of us.
Look at me and hear 1956 shooting out of my poodle.
See me eating shit, flail dancing at every sock hop.
See me parallel parking every Chevy Bel Air like a boss.

My Man.
My reservoir of kindness.
I'd steal plot specific things
from every movie set to make you laugh.
I demand a rewrite.
I demand your kiss, French theft.

You have stolen me in broad daylight.
You have a search light face
and it still shines hot
from my tiny palaces.

Then I plugged in the man.

His readout suggests:
CSSSSHHHHHHH.
Ribs. Bye bye.
CSSSSSHHHHHHH.
Scotch. Ow. Mmm.
CSSSSHHHHHHH.
Lady lady lady lady lady lady lady
cool buns lady lady lady
Lady lady.
My tandem swimmer.
My body pillow with veins.
Where I retreat and fall back in the war of myself.
Did you know all snakes dream of karate?
They wake up sobbing
and can't wipe the tears away?
Everyone wants a love
like a roundhouse to the neck
but not everyone is lucky in legs.
I dunno.
I'm crazy as a cranberry.
CSSSHHH.
I need to send a complaint letter to
Sharper Image for quitting too early.
Lady, I won't quit.
I'll marry your feet.
I'll eat 50 dollars.
You know I can do it.
I am psyched by your love.
I am also psyched by horseradish.
Shall I hold you like a ship's wheel
as the winds rise around us?

We should get some plants-
put 'em in our bedroom and when you sleep
I will watch them grow fast into your purple light.
My spectrum bright—
Fall back, fall back!
CSSSSHHHHHH.

No Purple

In the piney hills and apple orchards overlooking the Yucca Valley, stood the forever 1970s Oak Glen Christian Conference Center, Living Springs' high school summer camp. I was fifteen and felt too cool for the nerdiness of mountains but I secretly loved it. Camp made me miss the safe feeling I got from praying and it always seemed to sharpen my skills in figuring out how to speak in tongues without slipping into Spanish because even a little Spanish meant you were faking it.

Besides the reconnect with God, there were always three things about camp that I still liked: tender babes, crying and purple.

"Remember, campers. Boys are blue and girls are red, No Purple! Lights out at ten."

Due to me looking like an emaciated David Copperfield, I couldn't get anyone… in the real life city… to kiss me, but the compression of camp brought out the horn-dog, "Crazy For You" era Madonna in us all, so the odds were better. I loved passing a note at breakfast, telling a girl to meet me in the Sequoia prayer chapel and hoping to french her by luring her near with the power of close-up magic and if our tongues touched, we were boyfriend and girlfriend, for one full week. You could not get caught or you could be sent home.
No purple.

I also loved Cabin Devotion Hour. Cabin devotion was the first time I had ever seen other fellas be vulnerable and share their sins, missteps and fears. It always occurred one hour before lights out and was a time to share all that was buried inside, run by our 20-something cabin counselor. Five teens and one mentor spilling the heaviest shit you could never tell your own family, but if the hour was up, we would have to stop, no matter how hard the tears were rolling. Our bearded, vaguely Southern counselor opened up with a prayer and spoke low:

"Guys. I know we joke around a lot, and we are all tired from flashlight tag, but I want to encourage you to just…share your hearts. I want to talk about sex, like men."

Greg muttered, "With men? Killer."

"I'll pretend I didn't hear that, Greg. I am serious. As God looks over us, he wants to know our hearts. We shut him out of our lives when we clog the communication lines with sin. You know what liquid Drano is? It can kill you if you put it in your mouth, but it can open up plumbing that gets thick with hair and gunk. Who wants to open up the line to God again?"

Even though the analogy sounded like God would kill us if we put a dose of him down the wrong hole, we all raised our hands.

"Good. I'll let you know something. No one in the church knows this. I have had pre-marital sex, before I married Kelly." Jeff the young sports hero piped in, "Whoa. How was it?"

"It was awful, Jeff. There was no love. It was empty. It was sweaty, empty and kinda stinky. It was just like doing push ups."

"Push ups into a tuna hole." Greg was fearless. He told all the leaders that his Jesus and Mary Chain shirt was a promotion of Jesus and they let it slide.

"That's enough Greg. Yes it feels good. But so does marijuana. When marijuana is misused for pleasure, it kills. God gave us sex for a reason. Sex, for just pleasure, can kill you. It's meant to enhance a relationship, like parmesan on a pizza."

"Did you use a condom?" asked Jeff, eyes beaming.

"Of course not, Jeff. We're both Christians. Now. Have any of you, and I ask this with no judgment and it will never leave the longleaf pine of this cabin, have any of you been sexually inappropriate?"

Airwalks. New Air Jordans. Checkered Vans. Everyone in the circle stared down at their sneakers. I don't know why I was the only one scanning everyone's face for a give away. Greg piped in:

"I did. I had sex with Jenny. I know some of you at youth group were talking about it. I think she told her Mom. We weren't planning on it, but we scored some Boone's Farm Strawberry Hills and kinda went to town."

Greg looked fine as he said this. No remorse. No pride.
Like the best reporter, he said it like it was just something that
happened. I kind of wanted to be Greg. The counselor scooched over
and put his arm around Greg:

"It's okay buddy. It's okay. Do you want to tell God you are sorry?"

"I'm sorry."

"And mean it."

"I'm not an actor, Kevin. I sound the way I sound."

I really wanted to be Greg.

Counselor Kevin looked to Jeff, "This is about us and reconnecting
with all the good things God wants us to have and us turning away
from his fruits by being self-absorbed by sin and greed and sex. It's all
distraction. Look into your heart, I know the burdens are weighing
you down and you can share what you have been hiding."

The look into your heart line really got me. I was never a fan of
church lingo like encouragement, fellowship, born again or how's
your walk, etc.

I felt I had swallowed a canteen full of mercury. I had to get my own
heavy out, it was crushing me. I decided to share something with the
group, a sinful moment that only one other person knew about, that
had been eating me up inside. I was gushing and snotting
immediately as I recalled it.

"Guys. I love you guys and I want to first say sorry to God and sec-
ondly you all. I have been holding this in for a long time and I wasn't
going to share anything, because I know you all look up to me as the
cool skater Christian and I didn't want to let you down."

"What is it brother?"

"I…I…licked…"

"You licked?"

"I…I licked…a boob."

"Whose boobs?"

"Just one boob. Destiny's boob. At her house while Chastity and her Mom were at softball. I squeezed it too. With her top off. It didn't taste like anything. I got a boner and kept licking it and told her I wanted her and she said it was just lust in my heart and she began to cry."

"Because you knew what you were doing was wrong?" asked Kevin, warmly.

"No. Because I bit it. Buzzy told me girls like their boobs bit, so I bit it on the nipple and it hurt her boob. I thought it would make a little milk come out like in my dreams. There's no milk in there! Bigger boobs aren't big cause they have more milk. It's a lie. It's an empty nightmare of possible blood! She laughed at first and then cried. But I'll never do it again. I know I only saw one boob, but still, it hurts."

Greg put his arm around me. "I bet it hurt her more."

"Shut up, Greg! Not everything funny is a joke. Derrick. We forgive you brother. Say 'I am forgiven'."

"Not yet. I also masturbated to an Amy Grant album."

"Oh my Gosh. Which song?"

"Not a song. The album cover, the neon one of her that has the song 'Old Man's Hubble'."

"Good song."

"I know. I love her voice cause she sounds like she smokes but doesn't have the face of a bad person. I think she's hotter than Nicole Eggert and Alyssa Milano combined. I couldn't control myself."

With no judgment in his eyes, Kevin spoke steadily with his eyes on the floor. "That's how you know it's lust. Derrick. Let me tell you this. Amy Grant is hot, and it's okay to think that to a degree, but when you start sneaking albums into the sheets at night, or biting women on their privates instead of respecting them, you're sliding, bro.

We need to walk in a life that is as pure as Jesus was pure—and lustful thoughts keep us from being united with the Father."

"I know. I feel awful. I want to be able to communicate with God again. I'll do whatever it takes."

"You know what? You're gonna mess up again. You're human. The good humans try. And you can't try until you know all the things about you that are super gnar gnar. Who wants to lead us in prayer? And not Greg. I did not appreciate you sneaking in Doctor Demento lyrics into your last prayer."

"Wait," I said. I have one last thing I need to confess. I have been holding this in for so long, I just want the pain of it to go away. I…I put a ziplock bag full of shampoo and a little conditioner between two couch cushions and…I made love to it. I held the baggie and I dipped my thing and I did it. I made love to it. I was home, sick from school and…"

Everyone lost their shit, even Kevin, letting out the first howl. "I'm sorry D, but, but oh man." Greg was on his side, rocking back and forth, laugh-crying. "You screw furniture, dude! Oh I'm sorry…made love! We got a sofa pumper! Ha Haaa! A furniture fornicator!" Jeff couldn't even catch his breath from laughter, his face red as wet beets. "Oh geez, man. You need Jesus so bad, oh geez, you humped a couch. Ha! I can't breathe. I bet your wang is so clean. Haaa!"

These were deep belly laughs. I felt frozen and really thought I needed to get the dirty out, get it all off my chest in this safe space, but some things should remain secret. I eventually went from hurt and embarrassed, to hearing how cuckoo my words sounded coming out. I too began laughing until we were a drunk chorus. We all laughed so long and loud, I soon felt exhausted. I felt better. The laughter would die down, one person would look up at me and it would begin again, contagious. The door opened and the Oak Glen Camp manager poked his head in and clicked out the lights.

"Lights out now guys. Sorry to break it up. Keep it down, now until breakfast bell. Why are you guys cracking up? What's so funny?"

Kevin stood up in the darkness. "No reason. Just a case of the dude-giggles. And here's a random question. Does Oak Glen have a storage shed with a padlock?"

"We do. Why?"

"Because I recommend you lock up every piece of furniture you have, just in case."

Greg leaned up from his bunk. "Especially if it's cute."

"I don't get it, you weirdos. Lights out campers! No Purple?"

"No Purple!"

As we curled up under the sheets, chuckling, I laughed along with my friends, feeling like a weight had been lifted, even though we hadn't prayed, we just laughed the thing away.

Kevin said, "And hey, for real guys. This is between us. I swear to keep anything we ever say between us. No jokes. No blabbing. You have my confidence. All of us. Good night fellas."

"G'night Kev."

"G'night Greg."

"G'night Kevin."

"G'night Jeff."

"G'night Kevin."

"G'night Derrick."

Greg whispered, "Good night recliner sixty-niner."

I thought of word spreading through the camp about how I defiled the family room and turned our couch into a real bad scene. At the time, I wanted to die. Maybe the way Jesus wanted to die and leave this earth when he realized no one on this planet was ever going to really understand his unique take on love until he was gone. I'm not saying I'm better than Jesus, but I stayed.

THE AMERICAN GONDOLIER IN PROFILE
For Mindy Nettifee, after Strange Light

It is an easy sound that I miss. The slow easy sound of an oar moving through the salt water that I begin to miss like a ballad. The past always seems like it was easier than right now, and so I miss it. I miss the way the varnished oar spun in my hands and vanished mid stroke into the water, how the oar ground slowly at the cherry wood of the Italian fórcola, holding the oar in its curved arm, the big wooden, erotic curve of the hooked wood forcing the gondola through the dark water of Alamitos Bay.

I had been a gondolier for four years in the canals of Naples in the city of Long Beach at the Gondola Getaway. Some people think of only gangs, Bukowski, Snoop, Warren G, Dove Shack, Sublime, and an abandoned Navy town when they think of Long Beach. I think of small sailboats, fresh baked West Coast hip hop, poetry everywhere, dive bars, and Italian singing echoing from under the Naples bridges. It sounds like a purely romantic job: gondoliering all night, being a voyeur to lovers getting engaged in front of you at sea, singing Santa Lucia until you are ghosted and unnoticed, guiding tourists past mansions with docks, and dreaming of a better day where you too can zoom off to Catalina Island for a quick lunch of haddock and fresh crab.

The American gondolier's reality is a life of singing for eight hours to drunk guests who always want more, pushing your muscles to edge as you use only human power to thrust a heavy vessel through the afternoon gusts. Young lesbians tip great. Old lesbians do not. All gay dudes tip great. Teens who have a strange confidence tip great. All races from twenty-one to thirty-five tip great, unless you're a foreigner. Bachelorettes tip great unless there's an argument, and there usually is. White dudes and cowboys who won't let me help them into the vessel tip like shit. Wasted people tip great. The tip tells you if you can go drinking after and burn off the fog and chill in your bones. It tells you if you have to take a shitty side job to hit all your bills.

I took the job because I could choose my hours, which I was desperate for to boost my small career as a touring poet. I know how that phrase sounds, but after the army, I fell in love with poetry and needed a job that would let me bail when a good gig came up to do a live reading.

Every gondolier was assigned an Italian name: Bepe, Tyberius, Zamboni, Molto Benny. I somehow became Spaghetti. I was skinny and bad for you. It stuck. I was too skinny for the job, but persevered for four months of training and practice and learned that *skill*, not *force*, is the secret to moving the beast.

Gondoliering is not all beauty, cheese and Malbecs. Every gondolier has seen a couple try to do a sneaky blanket fuck where they pretend she is just sitting on his lap for old times sake. Every gondolier has been hit with water balloons by spoiled rich kids and only the best of the gondoliers park their boats and chase them down to scare the shit out of them. A man stood up to pee in the water in front of me. It's just an hour cruise. He said he wasn't sure if I minded. I saw a man propose by using the voice recording device in a Teddy Ruxpin bear. She said, "we'll see" and that was a long thirty-five minutes back to the dock. I saw a bartender tackle one of our fellow gondoliers in a pub, not as a surprise, but for twenty bucks, because the bartender at The Prospector said Tyberius looked like a dick in his work outfit. Twenty bucks is twenty bucks. The tables and chairs went every-where. They hugged, all fucked up.

I feel lucky to be filled with the stories from here.

Every gondolier has witnessed the amazing water fight that happens when the Filipino Catholics rent the whole fleet to celebrate Saint Clemente, the patron saint of water in one massive fifty person water fight, which we join in. Did I end up breakdancing on the large gon-dola, going from backspin, to top rock into a flying cannonball off our Carolina to soak the other boat? Hell yes I did. A bunch of us did.

I watched a woman drag her fingers through the red tide and the tracers of green glow as I rowed on was so moving. I remember getting a whole beach to sing "Rhinestone Cowboy" at the top of their lungs. I remember launching my beach cruiser off the dock into the water, thinking I could do a cool dismount trick mid air and could not. I remember a woman who was with a dude friend and when I asked them to kiss, she asked if she could kiss me instead and we full on frenched, and I almost crashed into the wall of the bridge. I remember the safe at the bottom of the bay, near the docks, with the bottle in it that new cherry gondoliers had to dive in and go find. I never found it. I remember the corporate man who cried when I sang Nat King Cole and wrote to me months later to say his bride walked down the aisle to what had now become their song. I remember going home so many nights inspired to write poems about the people I met, the good love, the love that had burnt out, the love that never was. The ones who would not kiss or look at each other. The ones who sang with me and shared their 'fuel'. The man singing gibberish while walking the canals every night. The ones who told me they had no money for tip but left me all their wine. I can not forget.

One afternoon, I was assigned a really old couple and knew the tips would be shallow. He looked like an Iowa farmer in his 80's and she looked like a British lady wizard from Love, American Style with her purple shawl, dyed red hair, and huge sunglasses. I watched them from the gondoliers shack, smiling while looking out over the sea, unfazed by the many knot winds whipping around their clothes. I loved their style. That's how I want to go out, wild. Wild in fashion and in spirit.

They came at a time when the winds were too high for my tastes, but not too high for the front office, and I was not looking forward to busting my ass through the gales blasting across the bay for two dollars. Once you got into the canals, there was peace, but it was a battle to venture in and out across the football field length of open bay between the dock and the canals near horny corner. But I got the call, donned my striped black and white shirt, my black pants, black Vans dock shoes, red tassled sash and made my way to work. No one stands out more than this white, old couple. I recall worrying that if the boat tipped they would just wave goodbye and sink. Weird hankies and teeth floating up.

I tried to recall our exact conversation when I got home. Here it is.

EXTERIOR – EVENING. CANALS OF NAPLES, CA, INTERIOR GONDOLA

DERRICK/SPAGHETTI is rowing an old couple, TRAVIS and CAMMY, through the canals. Travis pulls a blanket over his wife's shoulders.

TRAVIS
Thank the Lord the wind finally died down. Or maybe it's still roaring, and we are just blocked by the canals.

CAMMY
This really turned into a fine night. I don't even know if I need the blanket.

DERRICK
I know. Winds should be dead within the hour. Would you guys like me to sing? I know two songs in Italian and a Dean Martin classic. I also know the Alice in Chains "Rooster" song if so inclined.

CAMMY
Only if you want to, dear.

TRAVIS
It is your prerogative.

DERRICK
Really? You're the first people ever that have let me choose.

TRAVIS
We're all smiles either way. Sun setting. I got my girl and a jacket. All is well.

DERRICK
I'd actually rather not, if you're fine with it.

CAMMY
Just doing it for the tips?

DERRICK
Yeah. I get no joy from it. Little cheeseball.

TRAVIS
How come ya doin' this job if you don't like it?

DERRICK
I do like it. I like rowing. I like being at sea and drinking wine. I like
seeing the oar in the phosphorescence light up the water. But too many
guests expect me to sing, or demand it. Buncha pricks that think I'm
some Italian cartoon slave. I like doing things for people but not if I
get jammed into it. I still singsometimes cause I need the money, but
my heart ain't in it.

CAMMY
It doesn't matter if it doesn't have heart. When I met Travis,
I told him it was my favorite attribute, his heart.

DERRICK
I think if I heard a young couple say that, I'd puke, but you just said
that and it sounded sincere.

TRAVIS
She is very sincere. And true. Always has been.

CAMMY
Did you say I was a has-been?

Everyone laughs.

DERRICK
Did you meet online?

CAMMY
Oh hell no. We met during World War II. I was sixteen, and
he was seventeen. I was living in London and in no way
attracted to some soft doughboys.

TRAVIS
But then she met me.

CAMMY
That's right. I wasn't looking for someone in those times…and it's so
wonderful to be surprised by what
you thought you didn't want.

DERRICK

London in World War II must've been a scary time.

CAMMY

It was wonderful. We would go to the theater in Sloan Square…

TRAVIS

And the bomb alarms would sound…

CAMMY

And the theater manager would take a five minute break for those who
wanted to go to the shelter, to
leave.

TRAVIS

And no one ever left…

CAMMY

No one. We all stayed for the whole play, and could feel the theater
shake, and we would all burst into
applause on a big rumble.

DERRICK

Was everyone just kinda…not bright back then? No offense. I mean,
I'd hate to die, but I'd especially
hate to die watching some play.

TRAVIS

Not at all. You could die in the bread line, you could die in church…

CAMMY

You could die anywhere, all day and night, it didn't matter. So we
lived. We lived our tails off.

TRAVIS

That we did. Best time of our lives.

TRAVIS

Say Spaghetti, are we supposed to kiss under this bridge coming up?
I don't want to break
tradition.

CAMMY

And if you feel like singing, that'd be glorious. I'm sure it would sound massive with the echo.

DERRICK

Since you're English, would you like to hear some Morrissey or some Black Sabbath?

TRAVIS

Afraid we haven't heard of those crooners.

Derrick/Spaghetti rows them to a stop under the Ravenna bridge. We see the couple kiss and smile as Derrick croons…

DERRICK

Last night I dreamt, somebody loved me
no hope, no harm, just another false alarm…

CAMMY

Just lovely. Who is that?

DERRICK

It's Morrissey. He is the only British singer I can think of.

CAMMY

I'll have to look him up.

TRAVIS

Thank you for a lovely evening and the Morrison song.

DERRICK

Morrissey. You're welcome. You guys got spirit. I was glad to meet you.

TRAVIS

And here's a little something for you. Is this right? We've never done the gondola thing before.

DERRICK

It's just fine.

Derrick unfolds the two dollars in his hand, placed it in his pocket as Cammy placed her hand on Derrick's arm. Derrick helps them up the docks. A grateful smile slips onto his face. Scene. Derrick pedals home to his tiny ass apartment and writes a terrible poem while intoxicated.

He edits it into this:

STROKER OF SORROW

Pushing this boat through the slow easy,
black gondola steady
like a coffin
on a luggage carousel.

Everyone is in love on my ship
in love with the dark
because the dark is possibility.

No hard star glimmer above.
No sequin sorrow on the dresses of the horny.
Just slow stroker of sorrow
through the syrup of the canals.

Should I sing? I should sing. Tip or no tip.

Hoorah hoorah these ghosty places.
Hoorah hoorah the drunk calligraphy of two bodies unfurling
before me in a Mexican blanket.
Hoorah hoorah nervous laughter that feels like home.
Hoorah hoorah sudden lust and fumbling
for things on the floorboard
that won't be retrieved.

Slipping past the echoes of the Ravenna bridge.
All these mansions are bored. Money skeletons and mink blur coats.
The heads of animals
the ones they wished they could've killed on their own,
mounted for that unique kind of pride
that makes the knowing chuckle.
They will never play our music
in these mansions.

Stare at these sizzling and magic lovers before you,
their hearts full enough for the capsize of love,
down to fall for each other's full resume.

All hail these swollen weirdos
these bruised lip mongrels and misplaced lovers.
The ones born at the wrong time with the bowlegs and odd shapes.

The 'give this to me now or I'll eat your dumb cheeks' summoners.
The throaty kiss slingers who have waited so long for a
semi-private gush.

Fill this night with senseless acts of ha-cha cha. Go wild.
Say the first thing that you want as loud as you can.
So the last thing you want very quietly.
Hoorah hoorah that I just plain felt good tonight
among the tight arms of lovers.
Hoorah hoorah
that it is true as light coming from the water and solid
as this steady warming mansion lamps.
Heaven can keep 'em.

Someone is singing in confused gibberish.
Thank God he keeps singing our song.
Hoorah hoorah staying power you loyal dogs.
Hoorah hoorah the bridges puckering for our entrance.
Hoorah hurrah these echoes that are not forever.
Hoorah hoorah the night, the naked and poor
floating upon it.

NIGHT SWIMMERS IN THE AGE OF SIGHS

FOR DAVID MAMET, AFTER GLENGARRY GLEN ROSS

Let me have your attention.
So you're talking about what?

How you were crushed that they didn't realize you were
half night swimming,
half night terror?
Are you still hooked on tragic blow,
writing about somebody that doesn't want
what you're selling,
couldn't deal with the life you're locked into,
someone who moved on because the pussy was tighter uptown,
the dicks over at Saint Elsewhere were younger chimneys of endless
comfort
and you loved the ass of the past
so much more than the spontaneous fuckyes of now that
instead of going to war for what you deserved
you made coffee and held yourself and watched Silkwood?
Coffee and Silkwood are for closers.

Are you still wondering why even Jesus left you?
What a choice, to be invincible
and still ascend
instead of sticking it out with you
like a champ.

Maybe my phone will bring me love?
So you try and live in your phone.
Pretending that somewhere else is better than here…
Did you know that trying to get your mind
off of the righteous heavy of now
is for the weak?

Do you think I'm fucking with you?
I am not fucking with you.
I'm here from the nation of Texas and my death is rot-hot.
I'm here from Crimson and Clover.
I'm the hook and you will never let this death melody go.

As you all know, first prize for choosing to stay and fight
is a creamy face full of self esteem,
a rewarding miracle feeling
of being a maker.

Anyone want to see second prize?
Second prize is good vibes and a rain stick.
Third prize is who cares?
You get the picture, you dead drum circle.

You say you can't use the inspiration you're given,
You say "The Inspiration is weak." Thee inspirado is weak?

You are weak.
I've been in this business 22 years
ever since I got heckled selling my cassettes of poetry
when everyone wanted CDs.

They called me The Washington Post
because I was behind the Times.
How they booed me off stage and didn't buy my stapled chapbooks
at Jamz coffee shop in Huntington Beach
'cause I had merchandise but no conviction.

No one deserves to be heckled in Huntington Beach.

What's my name?

Captain Slothkiller, Admiral Juiced-on-wanting.
Emperor Carnage E. Hall.
That's my name!!

You know why, Mister?
'Cause you drove a 4 door bag of smug
to get here tonight,
I drove an eighty thousand dollar creamsicle.
That's my name!!

And your name is "you're waiting."
You little Footloose virgin.
You are scared to play in the Lord's game of creating and failing and
creating again because you think you don't know where to begin

and are too scared of the suck.
"Everyone else is a genius and has it easy.
I wonder where to start?"

You and all the new universes, pal.

Creation is a game of Gods
who are scared of why they, too, must fade.

And you go home and tell your dog
how hard it is to be hungry all the time and feel like you're gonna die.
But trust me, he gets it.

Because only one thing counts in this life!
Get them to feel something that is not a waste of their fading time!
You hear me, you former one celled spunk omelet?

You used to be the size of a comma. Get small again.
Then go monster up.

Create, Crash and Crush in this forage for blood.

Always be crushing!
Always be crashing!!

A.I.D.A.=
Attack?
Can I attack this idea with all my slutty guts?
Inspired—
are there angels drowning in the inspired song of my bloodstream?
Decision—
have you made your decision for Christ?!! Ascension is for bitches.
Stay!
Good doggie.
And action.
Raise the sails soaked in pitch and be war.

Fill your mouth with ginger and
kiss the old wallpaper away. Destroyer.

Come on sulfur storm;
Come on heavy barrel metal raining down.

You think the sparks came to your sorry ass to get out of the rain?
You are nothing until you burn for what you love.
Unless you love pedophilia.

Nice guy? I don't give a shit.
Good father? Fuck you—go home
and play with your spaghetti-faced kids!!
You wanna light 'em up? Heavy barrel.
You wanna feel your heart slip from faith to running face first
into the love of uncertainty:
Create like a sonofabitch!! No ones gonna like it 'til you're dead.
Good joke, huh?

You think this is abuse, you little meatless, cobb salad?
You can't take this—how can you take the abuse
you'll get from the interns at the LA Weekly?!

You know what it takes to sell the beautiful
and lost feeling of being us?
To create from nothing, risk your face and chase capture?
It takes brass labias. And that is pandering to the home crowd.
It takes guts to put your hand in the sparks
and say I do this for me.

You're ready or you're not.
You're the gasoline or you're a bunch of losers sitting around
in a bar in Huntington Beach comparing flip flops to toe shoes.
"Oh yeah, I used to be an artist, it's a tough racket."

These are the new inspirations.
What do we got here:

-On the handlebars, your foot gets caught in the bicycle spokes
and you lose a lot of blood
and you forgot that all that ugly inside is you.
-Fetal position yoga from the divorce you didn't deserve.
-You can't stop laughing during the funeral
and the more you try to hold it in
the worse it gets, as with everything.
-Your family begins making sense, finally,
when you're drunk.

-A force field comes when you blink twice,
every time you collapse remembering being struck by your provider.
-You learn to love losing the pillow fight to your sister.
-You're a ghost scared of being lost in the fog,
but fog feels like a family reunion.
-Instead of crying, you learn to pee it out.
-You break into the golf course and run through the sprinklers,
and as security chases you, you yell back
"where is my driver, who is my driver!"
-Your girlfriend finds your journal
and she cries, crushed by the worthlessness of your honesty.
-You start treating your love as an historical document
that will corrode in too much light.
-You learn to love your secrets.
-You stop looking for paradise in your partner
because paradise is just a sad strip club that gets boring,
no matter how cheap the prime rib and titties.
-You realize that Now is God and it's so big, it has to hurt.
You delete all your old timey filters on your camera phone. All now.
-You finally turn to a stranger
and say I love you…
and it feels so weird, but it is your last words.
-You stop analyzing how strange it is to weep at animated movies.
-You discover that purchasing your first strap-on in a store
and forgiving a close friend take the same amount of courage.

So,
you take action, you make action or you walk.
Greatness only demands declaration. I'm fucking great. Done.
You are great and the same time you are a pile of turds
and that is great.
You're only a fraud
when frozen by the constant debilitating wondering of fraud-ness.

And to answer your question, pal: why am I here?

I came here because Crimson and Clover sent me.
I'm a god damn death chorus, over and over
and I hope you hear me every time you feel dead to the cause…

because a God is a God,
whether famous, scared or fresh, whether seething away
in the clouds of silence or actively shaking the heavens.
Now is God. You are now.

Start a war, you son of a bitch.
Birth light.
Rename the beasts.
Make the snakes talk.
Bitch and nag the darkness until it concedes to your light.
Raise the bad sails.
Remember the approach of death.
Let that knocking push you to
leave a mark on this place,
your chance that the dead cry out for. "Just 5 more minutes?"
"If we had just 5 more minutes…"

Hear them hollering. Here's 10.
How will our sailing ships move
if we don't allow the dead
to fill the sky
with haunted sighs?
Be astonished by the ghosts you sense in the room.
Be astonished by the blood trying to leave you.
Be now.
Start a war.

WOULD YOU LIKE A MINT?

There are parts of Texas so isolated, so bereft of God, desperate as kitchen drugs, you could blow up a house and no one would turn a head.

I am far in the sunlight, floating in California. All the hard weather is gone. I am alone, at rest, at home on my Silverton fishing boat. Less teak. Docked between two large, wooden, remodeled sailing vessels. Gentle and deliberate summer. The book about Castro is open on my chest. Radio quiet, tuned to the Coast Guard channel. No emergencies. No one lost. The low daylight slips me in and out of sleep. No dreams. Salt is eating everything.

Breezes bang the metal mast lines.

I think of all my dumb needs. Mexican Coca-Cola, long women, things in threes. Pretending to be lost at sea is my long running joke. I keep telling myself I need to be alone but I don't go people watching because I loathe them.

I tried to build myself a life like a travel brochure life but I ramble as much as I always have. I have built a noisy life. This phone, this hard leash that helps me hustle to the next gig. My file cabinets are full of noise, things I am afraid to throw away. My mini-fridge produce drawer is a graveyard. I keep clothes and an air mattress at the office. I am pretending something is coming my way.

It is my father on the horn. His unmistakable Texas lilt. The sounds from opening your mouth less. He often skips over my questions or answers things I haven't asked. He's a dreamer. He always reminds me, "Derrick, this is your dad in Texas." I only have one.

"Hi. Hi Pop."

"This is your dad in Texas. You on your lil' ship?"

"What time is it?"

"So listen, I don't know if your Aunt Melinda told you, but your Uncle Gene has passed on."

"What? Uncle Gene? My Uncle Gene passed away?"

"He passed *on*. He has passed on. I'm sorry, if y'all didn't know. Is this a bad time?"

"It's not. I was reading. I was sleeping. Is everyone planning to come to Texas? How did he pass?"

"Well son, it is a complicated affair. The funeral *and* his death, I suppose. He was sick. He seemed to get better on his own gumption. We all visited him in the hospital and were downright pleasant to him. Some of us think he got to likin' the attention of the visitors, all hootin' and hollerin' their affections. And the fancy balloons. Weeks later, we think he missed the people and trays of food and the service, so we think he wanted a minor injury, maybe a head thing, to get back to that…and Ol' Gene ran his pickup into a ditch. He don't drink and it wasn't pourin' and he didn't love speed. Irregardless to say, he got a major injury. He has inadvertently made himself pass on. A kind of accidental suicide, I suppose. They say he went quick. I hope so. He didn't have a phone to call no one, so he coulda been in that ditch for awhile, 'til they found him. It's bad, son."

"Geez."

"Yep. Lord bless him. You never know how deep a ditch is. Poor son-of-a-gun. Are you coming to his funeral next Friday?"

I couldn't help but think of three things: Wanting attention, but dying suddenly instead. The feeling of crashing into something deeper than you imagined. What distinguishes a regular balloon from a fancy balloon.

"I want to be there, Pop, but I can't even afford bait right now."

"I know. I figured. And I'm sorry your Dad's not rich. I wonder maself how this whole thing is gonna go down, what with the feud and all 'tween Cecil and Melinda. Well, that's all the news that's fit to print. Everyone in Texas misses you. I mean your family. We miss you. I'll let you know how the funeral goes. May the Lord richly bless you. Bye now."

"Bye Pop."

More breeze stuff.

I pick up my book and think about calling my sister. I keep reading. Castro's beard is a real monster.

Fidel Castro was once asked why he always had a beard. He told the reporter it reminded him of his years with the revolutionaries in the hills, fighting to free Cuba from the conservative capitalistic dictator Batista. Castro said that if someone wanted to infiltrate the rebel hill fighters, he would have to start growing out his beard six months in advance to fit in. And no one in Cuba had that kind of patience.

Shreds of handmade blankets fall from the sky. Wooden splinters from an exploded rocking chair jam into the mud. All the burning photos unrecognizable, bubbling away to black like thin bacon left long on the grill.

Out of all my living Texan family members, Cecil is the most interesting uncle. He is also the most alone.

Uncle Gene, the one who passed on and away, was always the source of a sad, tight laughter, the nasally uncle who would mix up words so bad, you had to hold in your laugh out of elder respect, which always made it worse.

"For all intensive purposes, your skin look like you sat in a cacuzzi too long. Oaf-rah Winfrey did a show about how no one can excape germs in them bubblin' cacuzzi pools. Gang green and swimmas ear. I'd rather scoober dive in The Anti-artic."

Uncle Cecil, on the other hand, has always been the observer. I feel that in my own blood.

Cecil is the youngest of six siblings raised in a shack in the grassy slums of Cleveland, Texas. My half-Choctaw grandmother, Sadie Marzie Bush, had married a drunk, abusive, hard-working Irish man. They both loved Jesus with all their hearts. He died first. She laughed more and cooked okra. All six kids slept in one bed. Cecil was often picked on for being short. They messed with him good. They were all young and bored. He took every jab to heart. Something burned in him that no baptism could wash out. A kind of dare in the eyes.

Frozen venison spins like shrapnel, knick-knacks hushed into powder, a sewing machine dissected and falling through the tree line into useless thuds.

I feel guilty about not going to the funeral. But would I help the feud? Who needs me to be a shoulder out there, standing solemn in the blanket heat? How could a young tourist make things better by shrugging?

I go back to the book. I like it when I must keep reading, feeling the quiet war between my desire and my tired wrists. Castro was feeling trounced by the massive United States. In Russia, Khrushchev predicted that Kennedy would make a fuss about Castro, and then make a bigger fuss, and then concede. Kennedy launched a program to train 1,500 Cuban refugees to overthrow Castro. I imagine being Castro, thinking: That's it? That's all you sent? You tried to half-ass a revolution? You can never half-ass a revolution.

I envision the world leaders of that era, competing in a bloodletting contest to see who cried mercy or passed out first. Almost 200 killed in the Bay of Pigs invasion and the rest captured. It crushes me to hear about just one kid drowning in the Long Beach bay. I think about how beautiful and terrifying it would be, arriving on the island, gun in hand, ready to die in paradise.

America had stationed ballistic missiles in Turkey and Italy that could easily reach Moscow. Russia responded by sending long-range ballistic missiles to its new ally, Cuba. I try and imagine how I would live with a nuclear war always in the back of my throat. I try and imagine how it would feel knowing that a letter, poorly written, could set it off and kill millions. Everything important in my life—dust. I suddenly feel terrified of writing down a grocery list.

A bent skillet tumbles through the hot blue. Wood paneling puzzles across the field. Dolls zing apart.

Cecil was the only sibling to move his house a few yards away from grandma's house, right on her property. He spent the next several years taking control of it—building a pond, getting rid of the goats and cattle, and caring daily for May-ma. We would meet there on her birthday every year, the fourth of July. She had a laugh that could fill the Rio Grande and selective hearing.

"May-ma, are you gonna let Cliff ride that tractor with all them bottle rockets in his hand?"

Nothing.

"That's amazing about Brian getting married to an 18-year-old Democrat."

"Do whaaaaaaaat!"

When May-ma started to get sick, Cecil began to tighten his grip on when folks could visit. He wanted to be messed with less and left alone.

Kennedy and McNamara got spy intelligence from Cuban U.S. sympathizers reporting that large trucks with missiles were moving through Cuba. The U.S. called Khrushchev and asked if Russia was placing offensive weapons in Cuba, not noting that they already knew they were. Russia responded no. Always no. And to Russia, because the weapons were defensive, it wasn't really a lie. McNamara ordered a U.S. plane over Cuba to take photos, declaring that if it was shot down, it would be considered an act of war. Of course it was shot down. At this, a sorrow fills me. How often pride has trumped mutual devastation.

When May-ma passed away, she left her acres of land to Cecil and the house to her daughter, my Aunt Melinda. One day, a random phone call went out to all the siblings from Cecil: "If you want any of May-ma's stuff, you better get it now." We all thought he meant he was going to move in. We did not fathom that a week later, the house would explode in a not-so-mysterious gas and water heater malfunction.

Aunt Melinda once told me she dreamed about it every night. It was heavy on her.

I dream about it, Derrick. I dream about it in color. Everyone I ever loved is holding up the walls of May-ma's house. Pressing their backs to it. My family. Boyfriends. The gal who bags my groceries. I am hanging from the roof. We are encircled by men in black robes. No faces. A red bird comes and tells me to let go. I tell it I am afraid. It tells me to close my eyes and to let go with just one finger and I do. I lose my grip, fall and the house erupts. Dinner forks all warped and soaring. Her favorite plates with the presidents painted on them, smashed to bits, dropping like hail.

Dresses that made her feel beautiful, all falling rags. Everything moving slowly through the air. I am on fire but it doesn't hurt. The men in robes are ash and I am alone.

Melinda told me this with a face full of tears and pink skin. When she is angry, her accent turns up. "I will never forgive that greedy, heartless, Judas lovin' son-of-a you know what. Everyone is dying, Derrick. Your stepmom. Good brother Nolan. My dad—who had his moments. My wonderful, God-fearing May-ma. What can we do? How can any more be taken from us? How can someone not know how wrong they are, when so many are in a time of need? How could they think of just themselves?"

I tried to speak softly. "It was just a building, right? I know it was a special place, for all of us, but no matter how it happened, it is gone. Do you think it's time for our blood to move on, so we can do some kind of healing? Even if it is hard to do?"

Melinda adjusted her hem and said calmly, steadily, "Derrick, May-ma willed the land to Cecil, and her home, our family home, was willed to me. But Cecil got her to put the home insurance in his name. Don't you see? There is no place for us to gather and remember. The whole property is Cecil's now. He blew up our heritage for money. For privacy. For spite. He is friendly with the fire chief and we cannot press charges. He belongs in a nasty jail. I will never speak to him again. It makes me cry just thinking about it." Her eyes closed. "He is the unrelenting reminder that the forces of darkness on this earth are real and that Satan is hiding among us, closer than you think."

Years later, I still hear her words. Versions of her dream come to me. Sometimes I am the bird. Sometimes I am the silverware. Sometimes I am a camera perched in the middle of the scene.

The book is getting too heavy. I can only read a few more pages.

Khrushchev and Kennedy met in a Chinese restaurant in Washington, D.C. How could an arrangement be found in which both sides backed down, but neither appeared to—at least to their political parties?

34

The boat is rocking from the afternoon gusts and the natural light is travelling. I feel as though I closed my eyes and a week passed. I am at the office and the phone in my pocket rings. "Derrick, it's your dad in Texas."

"Howdy Pop. So…"

"Well just fine, thank you. Uh. Do ya got a minute?"

"I do. How was the funeral?"

"Well that's what I'm calling about. It was fine and everyone asked about you and I told them you were too poor to come out."

"Oh great. They must think your son is quite the success. Who all came?"

"Just about everyone. Everyone that's left."

"Even Cecil and Melinda?"

"Ohhhhhhh! I meant to tell ya. They did show up. I didn't know what would happen, 'cause as you know most of our family has carry and conceal licenses. But you wouldn't believe it. Cecil sat down. No one sat next to him. Even I shook his hand and sat elsewhere. Touched his shoulder. Two empty chairs right next to him and wouldn't ya know it, sister-baby Melinda sat right next to him, looking real nice by the way. She didn't speak for awhile. I watched them. Then she turned to him and said, "Cecil. Would you like a mint?"

"Are you kidding me Pop?"

"No son. I heard it clear as day. And Cecil looked at her, a little shaken, sitting in his new Sears overalls, ya know, and said, 'I would like that very much, thank ya.' He must've let it sit on his tongue for twenty minutes. And they didn't say anything else.
It was pure Jesus."

I go back to the boat that night and turn on the heater. I read that the U.S. agreed to never invade Cuba. They agreed to end the embargo and to pull their missiles out of Italy and secretly Turkey, which infuriated Europe. Russia pulled all their warheads and missiles out of Cuba. It didn't seem possible. It is hard to understand: dinner over Chinese food preventing this epic destruction. A letter inviting someone to dinner. What if the letter had been in an offensive font? What if it had been confusing or too poetic? Was it the soup that set things in the right direction? The perfect warm rice? The fresh duck?

The parties involved in the Cuban missile crisis, including McNamara and Khrushchev, met up twenty years later to c ommemorate the triumph of diplomacy over war. Angry men sit on their islands and get old. The Soviet Union is gone. Invasions in Cuba are over. The U.S. is still learning to talk. The bans on gays and religion in Cuba are lifted. Castro has turned to tourism. Everything is becoming something else.

A letter sent at the last minute.

A small mint, a gift that unfolds brightly on the tongue.

A change of breath in your brother's mouth.

Black Room One

The huge room is black. A soundstage, black. A long, black
ladder rises up to a diving board. Floors made of dry earth. No
pool. One light. You are climbing up the high dive. I'm too heavy
to get up. The muscles in my tongue are dead. I just watch you dive
and it takes five years for you to leap and fall through the sky. Your
approach, your body started in perfect form, now out of control,
flailing. You look at me like you thought I would catch you. I lift an
arm, not towards you, but to shield myself as you shatter into sparks.
It looks like stars being born in the dirt.

Black Room Two
for I. O.

The huge room is black. A soundstage, black. A black and white
ladder up to the highest diving board. He falls through the air slowly.
I am trying to cry as hard as I can to make him a pool, but it isn't
ever going to be deep enough. He smashes into 88 young songs, 12
unfinished paintings, 1257 bad jokes. It is all broken and can never be
heard by anyone. Some shrapnel lands in my mouth, and I can hear
a tiny sound when I bite into it. It says softly, get up now, open the
skylights and let the pool dry from the sun.

OUR BLIZZARD

I am running after her down thin sidewalks flanked by snow on 2nd Avenue and A, singing the midnight out, loose on straight Lagavulin, almost losing her in the veil of a Lower East Side blizzard. I am standing on the corner of a stalled Manhattan, cabs dead, no traffic quiet, panting, watching her go, hearing her high heel sprint in the skinny shoveled and salted sidewalks, fearless of slipping. I am not cold, watching it all come down slow over me. "Where are you going and why are you running away?" She does not look back. "Come and find me," she hollers. I run in the other direction.

I am far now, terrified in the cocaine cabin in the redwoods of Santa Cruz, hoping that someone comes to save me as the convict paces with his moustache powdered like a gas station doughnut. I am wondering if anyone will ever believe the Lisa and Leeza and Joel experience on the edge of the river Thames; the toasted, homesick Swedish missionaries quoting Bill Hicks to me, guiding me home as I felt the lights of London bouncing into me from the puddles. I am fumbling how to touch the sleeping young mother in the triangle shaped bed of my boat, who showed up unannounced in ripped fishnets and boots, who told me to not ask any questions and to make love to her like she was dying.

All the people who still sing after swallowing broken bottles.
All the camp counselors who earned their insomnia for the things they hide.
All the bug-eyed audiences of loving freaks.
All the haunted creeps of America holding you in the arms of their weed couches.
All the heart in the frat boy who shared his sandwich after I got jumped.
All the lovers who hated me because I sucked out the little they had left.
All the lovers who waited for us to meet again.
All the ice locked in the woman who kissed you with her hair loaded in smashed pearls of snow.
You're going to get it all and you may leave here empty. I am not going to tell you everything.

I wanted gusto, just like you. I wanted blood, love and travel, but I was too afraid to quit my job. I am still afraid, but I did it and I don't know if it's a better life. I got jobs off and on, but the spark to write was true because when the money vanished I had to keep doing it. I chased and hunkered down in the rambling feelings of my favorite books of poetry, to travel when I had enough bread and let myself be open to the anguish of falling for someone who lived far away. I wanted someone bright to come at me, and to come at me with spirit—to do the work on me. I knew they were waiting out there, somewhere. I wanted to feel the church of booze and debate, the church of no-guilt, the church of inclusion and anti-tragedy, the church of sexual madness. Didn't know how to get there.

I have been the biggest, self-conscious fuck up you have ever met in your life, degree-less, rambling on stage. I kept trying. It's all pass or fail for honky. I have tried to love with all of my red guts and blew it. I lived a life where pleasing others worried me so much, I was dead. Why don't they like me? It's no one's fault. I was a scared little wiener dog. I have inherited nothing but worry: no skills; no money; no craft. What I do have is insane perseverance.

I feel pretty lucky about the path I got to plow, the same road some of you will soon find. The bottom is where I am from and it is heavy and crowded. I am telling you these memories of the life, the wildish life so you may dip your toe in the only kind of freedom I have ever known. Soon, you will be swimming. Do not let religious repression stop you, as it did me.

I can't help but wonder if God is a feeling.

Travel far, sleep face down in every weed couch, perform your ass off and see the crowd right in their judging eyes, run, get lost alone, make out with the smokey throat one and learn endurance, lose your passport and dream of a new life, have the drugged up fellas in sandals try to slug you in Portland for saying cruise ships are better than bicycles, do it soon. You must be born again.

Every lover, every erotic moment on tour, every lapse in living is a plowed garden, a beautiful lesson and I recommend it fully. Here comes winter! Eat it all alive!

I loved the role of being a wandering traveler many could confide in. Troubadours who come into town for a short time and allow new lovers and friends to speak free of all guilt, history or suspicion.

I had to scratch the itch, ditch the past and see how art, poverty, God hunger, and sex changed me. I wrote down all the memories for weeks. The smell of Fisherman's Friend seasoning on her hands, the band Helmet playing while we blew each other, Cheese dog on a stick date, so much would remind me of the ones I had adored and lost. I realize now they are not lost, but waiting.

How did the dam break?

I left my seven years of useless abstinence and began fucking when a girlfriend demanded it and fell in love with getting lost in someone, in a moment. Then I was single and cruise controlled on Yes. I wasn't out to be glib with anyone's feelings or to see how many I could spray and conquer. I also wasn't some bullshit sex addict. I loved feeling like a student. I loved feeling wild, unlocked by someone else who made you feel needed. Lust was no longer the enemy. Lust wasn't just sex, it was a hunger for all things that charged the heart, new locales, old verse, kismet-everything. I had been afraid of becoming approachable.

I am telling you that there is much that awaits you out there, in sex and travel. Sex is not to be ignored or pushed down, nor is the spirit. Sex can be as easy as spaghetti. It can also be ugly and cheap and crushing. You gotta sort the other person's base. I needed it most after I learned it can be as powerful as any epic landscape and then pretty dumb. You have to get your mind, ego and heart to a good place first. If you don't, you learn, so it's not that bad. I captured my journey so you can know that you can do this. You are smarter than me. You have more skills and a choice. You think you're stuck, but you aren't. I pulled it off because I now know how to begin. If you hate your town, your love life, your job—you must go. You belong everywhere.

You never know what kind of saint or dirt-bag you really are until you can be still and sort out what happened. However, there was a lot of laughing. Art, sex and love. Why not chase it all the same way?

There she is, no longer sprinting away from me in the snow. I ran away from her for so long, I am now running to her. A long sunlight is falling on her face, pushing forth color, and in the beams, the chemicals rise in the steam of changing snow between us. I say,"Hello Beauty." She says, "I knew if you kept running, you'd eventually find me, you found son of a bitch."

CHROME HOTEL

The chrome latch wants to sing. It wants to sing off key
as I slide it to the side and stop the hotel door. It is beat, working
chrome, hard against the wooden door, chaffed and scuffed. Locking
the beam of hallway light into the room, small crack of splintered
light hitting the pillow next to me. Partner. She's not coming. This
is crazy. My heart is a thoroughbred in the last whipped lap. I'm
a nervous drunk with a credit card. I should just sleep. Close the
chrome latch. No. There is a pulse in the walls. The pulse in the wall
is shooting all its chemicals into me, the beige paint chemicals, the
former patron chemicals, my hands keep touching the walls to hear
lovers getting religious in the next room, their hands punching the
particle board, to scream the night away, the pulse is all tom drums.
The see the pulse of her in the ceiling stucco. How? How am I so
fucked up on someone so fast. I do not care to know anymore. I
just let it wash. I should sleep. I want to wait for her. She will never
come. It's too foreign. I could be madness. I could be lost and knifey.
I could be a broken engine who wants to touch someone without
paying. I should sleep. The night is wool. I strip down to my under-
wear. My body is tight with longing. I should think backwards on
my week, like a Scientologist and realize that memories fading is a
good thing. What makes me fade? What makes me vault my desire?
I should crash. I don't wanna go back in my memories all the way
to the womb. What sick fuck wants that bloodfood again? I should
forget her. I should close the latch. I will not fantasize about her more
than 2 more times. My hand sliding into my black elastic. I can feel
my warm. I can imagine her locked around me. Her leg lifting up by
her sweet face. My hands gliding down the rocket of that leg. I am
wishing her mouth to rush to me. To kiss me dead in white like an
avalanche. Rushing into the room and kissing me frantic like a scuba
problem. She is not here. Did I even tell her the room #? She has no
key. I don't know if she is dancing in the limp, spattered laser light of
some deaf DJ. Pressing her black skirt against the dead rafters of some
godless meathead. I should just close the latch and let the light in the
hotel room go from yellow sliver to solid black ghost. But I can't. I
want her to crack that door so bad, even if to say, I can't stay, this is
crazy. I'm leaving and I'm taking my hot ass radar dish. I close my
eyes. Morning is coming. It is not happening. Some fantasies are bet-
ter fantasies. They are stronger when wondered. I probably had too
much beer and would fart at the worst time. She is saving me by not
coming. I didn't shave. Anything. I probably still got coffee breath.

She probably has a jam band sex playlist. I will not see her shadowed in the Shining style hallway bulbs. I will not feel her sweating across my chest. I will not feel her lips dousing my neck and back. I slide my lids and fade fade fade. Then. The latch. She is straddling me. She has come like the warm storm you visioned up. You wake and wrap your arms around her like ship ropes. Pulled to the dock. She is wild, hair black as Catholic fashion. She finds your lips and all sleep is toast. You want her. She wants you, all of you. To crush and blitz. To moan and hush. To taste and warm and push. There are no dreams in this room and the pulse has dropped from the ceiling into this overly pillowed bed. Her body is now pulsing against the metronome of your body, syncing in clicks. You slide her to your face. Her pussy is a falling lake, a lake falling from the sky like the last days. You cannot stop tasting her perfect rush and long legged thrust. She is jamming her cheap cotton thighs around your cheeks. You pull her ass toward your face and your tongue is a search party. A brunette bonfire, a body shaped by arcs of electricity. She is moaning across the ceiling now. Her tits, a lust unwound, a fountain of please, please, please. I bite her nipples as she commands. I grab her ass as she commands. I fuck her until she can unload the day upon me. Cumming hard, wet down my thick cock. I will do anything she commands. I am lost in her chrome. Sing high the melodies of night. Fuck me she says. Fuck the shit out of me. You say, "Well, I'll try."

You find her legs. Dove bar smooth and soothing. Your cock as hard as a police baton, sliding across her panties, her lace black panties that vanish in the valley. This is all you are. Desire swallows. Desire true. She slides them panties to the side and lets you glide across the tease. "We shouldn't." "I know. We won't…"
And she rips me apart. I am inside her, a heavy unknown crush, a watching of the shadows around her mouth agape. Grinding her clit into the base of my cock, harder and harder, no pace, just loss of mind. She is moaning and says "fuck me harder. Faster."

You say, "I'm giving it a real college try here." You press your face to her neck. You smell the blood moving, you smell in the blood, the soil she came from. She says, "Now, fuck me beyond reason, hurry." "You want me to fuck you beyond sound judgment? Could be above my pay grade…"

"Just get me to cum, deeper, now, quickly…"

I see a flower, a marigold, push out from the top of her pussy...
and then two more.

"What's going on down here?"

"Shut up and fuck me faster, faster. I need all! Momma need all!" she
says with a chemical hunger, pre-programmed for sweat and gold in
that high siren of moans. It is a thing you have never had, maybe nev-
er again, that desire wreckage you have always wanted, that woman
wild and sure of herself, conjugal visit lust, the one is alive, giving a
banquet of nasty, the universe has pulsed through her signals from
the door latch.

Now, a marigold pops from each ear, one from her nose and a dozen
rise from the pores under her armpits.

"What the hell is happening?"

"Shut your little geek mouth and keep fucking me, make me cum, hurry!"

"This is some weird garden porn! There's flowers coming out of
your stuff!"

"Just make me cum you son of a bitch!"

"I'm doing everything I read in Sassy magazine!"

"Hurry, I have to cum now! Now! Now!"

I wrap my arms around her shoulders, her body under me. I thrust
and thrust, faster pumping, rubbing and sweating and pounding and
now...Marigolds shoot from her eyes. Her kneecaps, hundreds and
hundreds of flowers and stems from every pore. Thousands. The
smell of crushed flowers all over me, sticking to my skin. Then some-
thing gives away and I drop down to the floor—swallowed by just
fresh crushed flowers, orange and yellow petals everywhere. She is
gone. Not even a shoe. Looks like a pipe bomb at The Rose Parade.
Beautiful. Fragrant. Destroyed.

OUR POISON HORSE

ALL HAIL THE KINDNESS OF STRANGERS

What about all the friendly racists?
How will you deal with people not agreeing with you?
Are you gonna get a gun, a six pack of God, and a pickup truck?
Will it be weird not living around Asians?
Are you ready for the sun to kick your candy ass everyday?
How will you handle it when the lady at the DMV
asks your profession,
and you try to tell her "full-time poet," but she doesn't understand,
so she just stamps your application with the word
Pussy?

I only know this:
I moved here to Texas, where my father was born and raised,
several years ago.

The clerk at Target in North Austin saw my hands full and ran to get
me a cart without asking.

A bartender named Topaz at the Sahara Lounge asked if
we were new in town.
I sheepishly said, *Yes, like everyone else.*
He said, *Welcome home,* and I felt the murder of love in whiskey.

A waitress winked at me when I got a ringer playing washers
in the open air of Contigo.
It wasn't flirty. It said, look at you, you did something good.
I knew you could do it.

The past is all cast away and frosted glass.
Home is a feeling.
All hail the kindness of strangers.
You can handle the weather anywhere if there are good people.
Maybe too much good weather makes great people bad.
Maybe bad weather
makes it feel like
we made it through something, together.

To my friends in the West:
I have found there's good and bad everywhere you go.

Maybe everyone is nice in Texas
because it's so easy to shoot someone in the face
if they're not nice.
Oh, and
I own two guns now.
You gotta come visit.

THE STARGAZER IS DYING

And I'm telling you to live, to hang on.
I'll change the low water in your vase.
We can jam you back into the ground.

Spring is in approach.
The squirrels are being photographed.
There is a flood of sunlight coming.
The rivers are rising for swimming.

Why do you give such sweet smells
before going?
This color and slow leaving is all you get to do?

You made the dead house wonder.
You made this gaze bloom.
We carried your beauty to others
and said,

Can you imagine seeing this in the wild?
Can you imagine how beautiful
it would be
if it were still alive?

GRACKLES IN WAR LIGHT

I have never seen the light swallow
the field like it did last night.
I couldn't leave the barn.

Have you ever seen lightning dance that fast,
so pissed and ready for death,
the night goes all hard-on, strobing along,
wanting to take some farmer down?

I wished I could go into the clouds
and watch from above: the descent
of all the bright war light,
imploding gods,
angelic powder kegs alight,
howitzers hammering down over this little
yellow
barn.

Soon, the storm holds and the grackles
perch on the barbed wire. Unmovable.

The wind winds down
in surrender.

A battered black chair has landed in the field.
I can't help but think it is for me.

If I sit upon it,
will the winds rise?

The great oak
leans alone on the hill, staring down
the field, full of blood-thirsty birds.
How can there be so many vultures
and still so many rabbits?

The grackles take audience with the vultures.
One vulture lifts from the tree,
wings as wide as Christ,
and holds fast in the headwind, still

and high, frozen in the air,
head down,
feathers rifling.
Dressed up
for the occult hazing, he goes nowhere.
Just holds.
Not hunting. Floating post-storm.

A break from the constant job
of waiting out the weather,
waiting for food,
for blood and murder,
for carcass and pickings.

I swear he is having fun.

Yes, the other vultures never understood him,
watching their special brother with disdain
as he does nothing in the low gale.

How they wish he would stick to his role
and wait for the lightning to take down a beast
so they could fill their bellies and live a life
of waiting for something awful
to feel full.

THE RUINED LIFE

Your life is ruined
when one lost person becomes a loved, low song
and you stop searching
for new music, convinced it will all sound the same.

Your life is ruined
when you hoped the violence
you saw in him
would protect you from the world, and how sad that it did.

Your life is ruined
when someone makes you choose
science or miracles
without seeing how well they party.

Your life is ruined
when you realize too late that the magic it takes
to change someone
exhausts all your magic.

Your life is ruined
when you begin to rebuild your home
before the last bomb falls and the war
is declared over.

Your life is ruined
when people holding hands
while riding bikes
just seems dangerous.

SOUR MASH

and so you hit the road with some other white poets
and you washed diner dishes in Dallas for a discount on your meal
and they passed the hat around the audience
and you made 50 bucks
and you bought everyone pancakes at Norm's
and years later you hit the road alone
and they paid you 200 bucks
and you bought yourself a flask
to make it through the long open mics
and then you hit the road
with a queer author and a black dude
and they paid you 1500 each.

and you knew you could make a go of this poetry thing
that sucked at your chicken legs and made you follow
and you saw yourself changed
and you thought this kind of art form
could be medicine
and not just embalming fluid.

and you and the power blonde
put on shows in aquariums
and the audience said they loved it
but they didn't buy much
and you only sold two shirts and three books
and you tried going big
and began opening up for rock bands and comics
and you learned that dancing and laughing
had a higher market value than your metaphors
and you took the gigs, all the gigs as the gorgeous
talked through your sets
and licked the love in their phones
and you took the job reading your work at the Chicago party clubs
and read to a loud room that
mingled around the images that broke your ass
and your stack of ideas sold nothing as someone told you
that you were great ambience.
Ugh. You never wanted to be ambience.

and you applied for the grants
and wondered what you'd get to do
if you
won them all,
but you lost them all
and didn't know most of the words
in the winners' proposals.

and the publisher
thought you were sexist
because you wrote the poem
about eavesdropping
on your ex-girl during her new date
after seeing her car parked outside of what was 'our bar'
and as she spoke low of you, you hot crawfished
and you were the creep that just listened
like a scene from Mannequin 2, it stung 'cause it was true
and how you couldn't wait to write down the poison
that kept yelling like
a dog locked inside a four-door summer
and the publisher tried to teach
you that real life sells, unless it comes across as needy
so go learn the easy truth
that makes people cheer.

the truth between strangers:

respect. the weather.
listen to how we feel about the weather.
write about the moon
but not about how it fucks up our blood.

and no one wanted to
risk their book sales
by talking about what we all
talked about at the bar.

you all lied to the interviewer when she asked,
have you ever had a racist thought?

have you ever had a million thoughts at once?
have you ever wanted to murder someone with a huge smile?

have you ever realized you were lying about love onstage?
have you ever wanted to die because of how you used to be/are?
have you spent more time writing about living than doing it?

and some of you and your friends got so turned on
by the hunt for the evil people in your scene, the detestable,
the black energy of losers,
you stayed erect for days
and wrote 'everyone else is wrong'
with your gleaming cocks and perfect nipple ink.

and some of your friends realized that loneliness was power
and they slipped away.

and some of you and your remaining friends
kept writing inspirational
'hang in there' pieces
'cause the rest was too hard to live off of
and the nasty was making us lose fans
and we didn't write anything truly broken, scary, fuck-heavy, cheap
or dirty anymore
and we justified it because we really wanted this one bastard art form
to reach the masses and change the world,
or at least a township
because we thought it was better, it was now,
we knew a great line of poetry was a bullet
and novels were a long choke
and no one had time anyway for real phone calls or involved dinners
so we nailed the fast power of today by turning to poetry
but we poets only argued online amongst ourselves
and pretended that it mattered.

we glowed like we could change the world from an anonymous laptop.

the reviews came in:
your poetry didn't change anything—
it just mentioned the monsters
and moved the monsters
to the other side of the room for someone else.

you thought about real estate sales and finally eating well
you thought about sheep wrangling residencies where your hands
become soil
you thought about being a motorcycle mechanic
that actually fixes something—

anything to feel real and stop wondering
about capturing all the 'you don't know what.'

to fuck when you want to and not
ponder the beauty.
to drink when you need to
and not unlock the diary.
to wander in the woods and not
look through the pines
for a great closing line.

to have an internal fuck you every time
you look at trees and say
yes, they are beautiful...but they are huge, unmovable, wet and living.
what does that mean about me?

morning dew ain't day tears
storms are not angel farts,
cum is not the dying, drying frost of love.

you used to think poetry was important only to poets,
and now you know that isn't true.

poetry is important to few poets
is true,
as you loom in the libraries of your fellow writers
and notice that if they own more than 10 poetry books
almost everyone is dead.

writers have a hard time
loving now. So, go.

close it all down.
close it all down
and finish the applications.

then, you get a letter.
someone says they *needed* one of the poems you wrote.
not that they liked it. Needed it.
you try to laugh it off. You try to say you are making
a little lost thing important. The way the bones of a child
found in a lake can't be easily remembered as a boy.
you try to see something cynical
in how you feel reading the letter.

but all that comes now is
you feel like taking out the trash—
you feel like taking out all the trash, everyone's,
and even though you don't know how to—
you want to skip around like an idiot

the great amnesia sets in. and it's back to—

hello, blue bonnets swaying across wide Texas.
hello, all you animals flying above in the blue, blue laundry.
hello to the quiet someone
who removes darts
from the other side of night
and leaves us with
the many little holes
of surprise light.

300 Bones

Roy Sullivan still holds the record
for being struck by lightning 7 times
over the span of 20 years
and surviving. He left this earth by his own hand.
The lightning could not take him down.

I can imagine the first time it found him.
Out in his pickup truck at night,
remembering that a truck can diffuse lightning
but not if the window is down—Vajam!
Feeling the first blast of light wash over him fast
like a fire hose gushing electricity, turning him all X-ray,
hands steaming, hair sizzling, heart shock-jacked,
hot organs huddled up,
a left hook from the heavens.

The second and third time it struck him
it all felt sudden and ridiculous.
An impossible stroke of luck.
The news trucks showing up.
Mr. Lightning Rod. The Human Conductor. Roy, the Lightning Sucker.
Priests in their hickey hiding collars, using his tale as allegory,
telling kids that God physically punishes the wicked
when we step out of his love.
The fourth and fifth time, people distanced themselves from Roy.
Scared of the ire he drew from the angels
and all the forces of heaven.
Roy was gunpowder.
He was a marked target.

His boots flying from his feet.
Laces still tied.
A jug of water to douse his burning hair,
always at the ready in the passenger side.
His wife leaving him after he was struck.
The news turning his magic common.
The sixth time. No one came.

Roy's fingernails black and gray. A scar down his shin. Hair crisped.
The doctors gave him aloe vera and told him to be careful.

They couldn't explain why he wasn't dead.
Roy moved through the town like a ghost
even when the sun was shining.
No return to normalcy
when the world christens you as bad luck.

The seventh time.
Roy noticing thunder clouds rolling towards him,
daring them to speak. "Try and take me. Try and take me away."

A smile welling up in his burnt molars when he feels it
start to sprinkle.
It strikes. It bullets down, whips his legs out. He is unconscious.
His suspender buckles, like stoves.
He pulls himself through the mud
to the passenger side of his truck,
dumps the water on his head.

One reporter returned to the emergency room:
"7 times, Roy. Aren't you scared that you've pushed your luck?
Most people die from one.
Will you still go outside to work if there's a storm?"

Roy replied in simple Southern notes:
"I will still try to."

The reporter whispering to Roy, "What was it like?"

Roy sitting up and clearing his throat.
"What was it like? It hurt. It all hurt.
The lightning and everything leavin'.
But I'm glad it happened.
I feel strong. I feel strong the way you feel strong from new love,
and I see now that I can't go
until I get it all out. I am so full.
I have to get it all out. If God wants it back,
he picked the wrong fight.
It's mine.
It has always been mine.

My heart beats on.
My bones are strong.

Five times stronger than steel,
not poetically—scientifically.
We are born with 300 bones, and we die with 206.
This means
there are bone guzzlers in the shadows.
All dressed up in No, thank yous and Get losts.
They will come for you,
and you must douse them in jars of blood, cum, flowers, yes, color,
fast power, truth stripped, hard loss, tongue kissing, sorrows bazaar,
flight, love, love, love, and 100,000 beats.
Money broke up with me a long time ago.
I stopped reading the Bible
and started believing in miracles—
alive is a miracle. No matter how jacked.
Your life is medicine to someone.
You gotta go find the sick.
Do I still dance like a sicko even when I witness
all the great dance halls are closing down?

One dance floor closes down
and I see the streets open up and the canals freeze over
and the rooftops get ready
and the backyards of night are lighting up
and the basketball courts get ready for stomping
and the empty bars are turning up the music
and the abandoned buildings, all dressed up like us,
are broken into and lit up like New Year's fireworks over Iceland
and we still dance.

Will you still dance
when no one needs to dance with you?
That's the war. When everyone is done with ya.

Lightning is striking somewhere, all the time.
Wait for it to roll towards you, across the horizon.
Feel your bones ready for the light to burst upon you.
Bones will be all you feel, it is all you are at the end.

May your radios be too loud.
May you lose your voice singing the road trip eternal.
May you stand fast in the crushing storm when there is no shelter.
May you challenge the heavens.

May you dance on the wreckage after dismantling the myth
of constant hell.
May you dance the jaws of life.

Great power comes at weird times in the strangest places.
Winston Churchill was born in a woman's bathroom
during a dance.
May you enjoy the courtship
and hail its sudden arrival.

May you dance the dance of the unknown.
May you get the hell out.
May your heart move you so wild
your love
scars your legs."

LIBERATION BLUES

Of course, the French waiter was skinny—he was French.
He had a slight Aussie/Parisian accent, which is a strange soup, but
Canberra is home to the strange and the new.

The American-sounding blues band kept playing after my reading,
nailing SRV into the lobby walls.

Of course, I was exhausted and wanted to loosen the feeling that
comes after you shake too many post-show hands to feel sincere.
Of course, I wanted more Tasmanian whiskey and an Aussie Rules
Football match in my room to unwind alone at the perfect
Hotel-Hotel.

Of course, the Frenchie came up to me and asked if he could
give me a hug.
Some fans do this, and there is either a true sweetness or it feels
like a dare.
Of course, I thought him to be a chiseled tipsy fella taking the piss.
He looked like a spy.
And he was French.

I asked him why he wanted a hug.
He asked if it was true, if I was in the 82nd Airborne.
I said yes, in the '90s.
He said his grandfather lived in a village in the north of France
liberated by the 82nd during WWII and that his grandfather said if
he ever met an American paratrooper to give them a hug because if
not for them, he would not be here, nor his father, nor him. He held
out his arms and said, so thank you for, in a way, letting me be here.

Of course, I hugged him and told him I didn't do anything.
He said I was the first American Paratrooper he'd ever met,
so it still meant
a lot to get to say thank you.
Of course, his eyes welled up.
Of course, I was ashamed that I didn't feel anything.

Of course, we shook hands post-hug, and I packed up my gear.
Of course, I went out alone
and got hammered on beer and strolled, blasted silly,
until I ran out of the colorful cash
and felt nothing.

I listened to the music playing over the lake
and felt nothing.

Of course, when it all wore off,
I looked up into the night air
and looked as far as I have been allowed
and cried like a lost child.

THE YAWNER IN THE BACK OF THE VENUE, ROLLED EYES, THE EDUCATED SMILE, THE NUDGED RIBS, THE SENTIMENTALITY; SENTIMENTALITÉ AND MELODRAMA PUSS, LENDER OF LEFT HOOK, A SOFTNESS; ZACHTHEID! AND OUR WILLINGNESS TO BE SUCKERED

Naomi was bored by poetry
but still went to the readings at the Rosenau in Stuttgart to watch her friends'
attempts at "filleting" their emotions.

Derrick, would you and Joel like to come to a house party?

We would love to.

Okay, but no talk of poetry.
I don't want everyone to kill themselves.
At the party, a local author told me that my poetry absolutely blew him.
I also learned the value of eating well on tour, as an artist told me
that once a week I should splooge on a good meal.

After drinking to the point where we sang
Springsteen in high heels,
someone suggested we hike into the hills
overlooking the city.

When the others got out of site,
Naomi, the tall, gorgeous, disinterested one
who seemed more like a mistrusting nurse,
slammed me into the wooden fence,
smacked me hard across the face like an old-timey duel
and kissed me. She kept doing it,
fighting to get her hands free as I struggled to clench them down,
as if each smack would be soothed with a harder kiss.

It was bizarre, fantastic, and super German.
It was the strangest payback for World War II.
I loved her throw-pillow lips.

I'd like to see her again, just to catch up over a Obatzda and a Radler.
Are you married now, Naomi?
Don't answer.
I will just look around the bar
for the fella with the most
blood pouring out of his face.

I can't forget
lying in the dirt covered sunrise,
wanting to move there to be with you,
live a life where I had to tell strangers daily,
"Um. I fell."

Awake at 5:30 a.m. is always a story.

Wine sent us into the darkness.
We talked about the future.
Nothing much came of it.

Beautiful correction.

Wir befaßten uns der mit Zukunft.
Wein sendete uns in die Schwärzung.
Nichts kam von ihm.

Favorite Roller Derby Names I Made Up in Portland at Claudia's Bar While on Tour; unclaimed so far

for Juliet and The Rose City Rollers

cruela da skill

her majesty – queen elizabitch the duece

rink witherspoon

princess slaya

crash bandikooch

miss guided missle

brasby skills and bash

babe-rahamber tamblyn and the sisterhood of the travelling blood-bath

mary tyler morgue

boobie howser, m.d. (math=death)

florence henderscum

aborshauna

boob marley and the wail on ya's

Lisa

Places You Should Never Kiss

1. In a Men's Warehouse, not the suit store. A warehouse where they make lousy men.
2. Conservative foam party. Not right wing conservative, conservative as in the soap is rationed so no one gets too fucky.
3. On the Peter Pan ride at Disneyland. Don't real kiss while fake flying. Notice how you move over the darkness. Pay attention to tiny London. Tiny London is paying attention to you!
4. At a gun range after happy hour. Everyone you love is one joke away from heaven.
5. In front of someone in Malibu with a sense of humor.
6. In a gay western seafood bar called Fish and Chaps.
7. You should never kiss someone who is trying to enjoy a churro. A churro is just a donut with a boner.
8. During a conversation at a party full of comedy improvers, and every conversation is powered by the improv rule "don't deny." So yes, I WILL have another drink and everyone will yes, wear their church pants into the above ground pool; and yes, you will drive me home in a new un-cynical life of wet pants, bonus drinks, and learning to say yes. Put a towel on the seat. Get me in it. Take me home. I'm outta words. I'm blanking. Kiss me long war. Kiss me like Hawaii being born. Kiss me the opposite of cross fit. Kiss me Tennessee porch song. Kiss me assy. Kiss me dead as drugs. Kiss me lost. Kiss me gold in the boozed up sunrise. Kiss me all the way home.

MENDER/DESTROYER
for the best of friends, Cristin O'Keefe Aptowicz

Cristin and I were chatting
about her breakup, her new life
how everything was brand new and then—

        her chair broke,
and she fell to the floor
like mashed potatoes.

She didn't cry.
She just laid there, stretched out
and looked like an extra waiting
for action to be called in a catastrophe film.

When a poet eats it, they begin sorting out the meaning
of all broken chairs,
of all support
surprising you
and caving in suddenly,
unsure of
what sucks more—the bruise or
having to check chairs for the rest of your life.

I helped her up. Swung open the glass door.
I threw the chair high into the backyard air
and watched it shatter.

"Fuck this chair.
This chair is from the forest of assholes.
This chair can eat my hot fuck and die."

Cristin then quietly went outside barefoot,
collected the pieces from the grass,
and took it into the garage
so she could fix it.

"It didn't break.
I broke it. So I can fix it."

Seeing Blood in The Ocean

"Built for the arts of peace and to link the old world with the new, the Queens challenged the fury of Hitlerism in the battle of the Atlantic. Without their aid, the day of final victory must unquestionably have been postponed."

—*Winston Churchill*

Is that Emily's blood? How strange that
blood is alive. I can't wrap my head around it.
Blood is alive.

We were swimming at sea off the stern of my boat,
and somehow
she cut her leg on a screw.
As the others on deck cared for her,
I stared into the water.

I wondered what the blood would draw forth from the bottom.
I recalled that I always swim underwater with my eyes closed.

How many conquered Navies do we swim over when we
close our eyes and submerge into the sea?
I am imagining all the coral covered cannons from sunken ships
opening up their breaches, sending bubbles to lure me down.
I imagine the brackish water eating soft bags of men fading in the
sand below, their colors rising up and churning in the foam.
What all am I swimming in when my eyes are closed in the salt of the Pacific?
Little bones. The dirt and elements of man. The hungry salt.

I see the great tourist ship in the distance, the old *Queen Mary*.
Ocean after war.
Ocean after war is in us as we swim.

The Grey Ghost, the *Queen Mary* ship left them all to drown.
Faster than any U-boat, the speeding mammoth
had to zig-zag so she would not outrun
her protection.

She mistimed a zig and smashed her bow
through one of her own cruiser ships, the *Curacoa*,
cutting the other vessel into a graveyard.

100 men, alive in the water, waving their arms
and white sailor caps
for rescue.

Horror filling their eyes as the Grey Ghost made a choice and
left them all to drown so that the 50,000 others may live.
There would be no rescue. The mission to the UK must go on.
Was it worth it?
Not when you are in the water.

Whenever someone tells me it's hard
but it's the right thing to do,
I am in the water.

Emily, I don't know how or why it works,
but the salt water
will help stop the bleeding.

THE WANDERING HOW

Green easy,
hunching hills of Germany.
Blue glass,
glacial jags of Austria.
Snow slushed,
streets holding out for curd gravy in Vancouver.
Tight bridges,
lost on Campari and midnight Averna, rolling over high tide bridges
of Venice, Italy.
Stubborn tundra,
sled huskies with ADD, pissing while running, racing over virgin
Alaska.
Jarred fireflies,
the grocery on home street in Atlanta where the music is fresh-power
and hollering.
Autumn crisp,
kids napping safe in leaf piles near Dartmouth.

I am home on the road.

Sweetness awaits,
open arms of non-war, foreign beds, dinner parties ready to unravel
the headlines,
a freeing love in the sheets of strangers, to share our common
darkness
and not bloat.

The right feeling when it is time to get gone.
How right lost at sea can feel,
How you learn to walk less muggable,
How you will be smashed in the dome by the surprise axes of love,
How you refuse to be crushed by the empty air of
"what if I still suck,"
because it doesn't matter.

A rucksack full of grit,
a heart compressed in a hostel bunk,
the tone of voice coming from a locket,
told you to keep pushing up the hill.
Was it Kate Bush?

No matter how broke, how jib flipped, how outscored,
how hungry you get—

you realize that all this touring is an epic attempt to impress your
Mother.
Thank you is un-poetic.

Thank you.

TONGUE ON THE WALL

"No one should outlive his power."

—*John Davidson*

Being forgotten is not as bad
as hoping you aren't.

A bridge crosses the Mississippi.
Berryman stands upon it.
The bells speak.
Feet first.
Beard flipping up
like a tent flap in the breeze.
Jumps.
Misses the water.
Hits the bank.
Classic Berryman.

Hard earth is less scary than dark, forgiving rivers?
Because the soil could push out
what you couldn't?

I write in a library of a dead poet,
a remodeled home in Lenox, Massachusetts
and I don't know any of the titles on the white shelves.
We are so unknown.
I feel dumb in grief
as last week when I saw the first book I ever wrote
in a used bookstore
for a dollar.

I wanted to cry. I tried so hard. All these books tried so hard.

Now I want to stop, not because someone
abandoned my work, but because
there is just so much
and it really ain't nothin'.

Someone kissed me once and bruised me good and it ain't enough,
and I know what a snowmobile feels like in mid-air and it ain't enough,
and I got lost in sunlight on an island and found unopened wine

and it ain't
            enough.
I have a couple of good dream songs that are my best but they are
leaving me
and it ain't nothin'.

John Berryman's Dad,
shotgun blasting his tongue onto the wood paneling,
how that photo repeated on every page of Berryman's books,
the end of language,
the end of Boy.

John are you whispering:
"you folks just don't know. You just don't know
yet."

Poetry didn't take your life.
It kept you here.

It kept you here until you closed your eyes
to the spirits from smokestacks, to the lawns of America
and grew away from the power of swallowing songbirds
and the hissing fuels of night. You turned away.
Not us.

Did going inside kill you?
I hope you missed the river on purpose.

If you dig at a foundation for too long
the home
will collapse.

John, John, over-read John.

Being forgotten is not as bad
as hoping you aren't.

I hear the thing you fell for every day
and shove you back down.
Stillness,
stillness
ain't nothin'.

SCIENTIFIC AMERICAN

Every time a poet
uses the word
'soul'
hell expands,
just enough.

CAKE WEEK

We visited the grave again and this time
she lay across the plot,
trying to hug it, trying to will herself into the ground.

I couldn't believe it still broke her up this hard after so many years.

When you accompany someone visiting the grave of a loved one,
and you stand there, next to them,
looking for your own last name on a tombstone
it's 'cause you don't know what to do or say.
You try to not look bored or distracted, you try to show sympathy.

You hold her and try to tell her that we love the spirit and not the flesh.
Their spirit is always around us.

She will tell you that you are wrong.

Both, Derrick. I miss Both.
It's like a painting. We don't love Matisse's paints.
We do love what we saw, what we held,
and we can also be amused by how it got there. The spirit is just paint.
You would always rather go to the museum to see a painting
than try to appreciate it in a book. It might make me feel good to say
I loved his spirit, but I love both. Flesh and whatever it is that
I am calling a spirit for now.
I loved his woodshop hands. I loved his steering wheel chipped tooth
and skin that looked pulled down by barn pulleys.
I can miss what I can't see anymore.

What a fucking joke that we have to go away.

It's like giving someone coconut cake
and it becomes their favorite thing
and then someone says you can only have it for a week
and then never again.

Yeah, but how good
is that week
of cake?

You Will Be Destroyed in Your Own Way

All the pictures I tried to take were too sudden
and poorly framed.
Half-faced soldiers.
Blurry telephone poles.
Too much ceiling, not enough body.

I'm 18 and don't know how to plan a shot.
I feel a thing, and I grab the thing
that captures the thing
and shoot.
You must be quick on the draw
because everything goes away
so fast.
I shoot with confidence and
confidence is nothing recognizable at 18,
nothing is recognizable.

I'm constantly making the world's worst film:
young men in green, same haircut,
loaded down with the loneliness
of dying towns.
The world won't remember their names.
Me neither.

They are going through the tear gas chamber today.
You have to take it all in. Mouthfuls.
You have to let it destroy some of you
so you can have confidence.
There is no other way.

No one wants to be the guy who can't control the snot,
how it flushes flood, gushes like a storm well.
No one wants to be the guy who pisses himself
crawling under M60 tracers.
No one wants to be trembling clumsy at the grenade training,
throwing a pin down range
and blowing your and the Drill Sergeant's legs off.
No one wants to be the God who believes we would all make it,

the guy who cries when the mail doesn't come.
You wanna be a man,
but you got no blueprint.

Here at the chemical weapons shacks,
the gas gets us all in some manner.

Remove your mask, and yell your battery's motto:
"Mad Dogs, Mad Dogs, we got guts!
Mad Dogs, Mad Dogs, we kick butts!
1st platoon, second to none, if we can't do it, it can't be done!
Drive on, Drill Sergeant, drive on!
Drive on, Drill Sergeant, drive on!
Dogs—YO!—Hit 'em hard! Woof woof woof!"

We stand in the yellow smoke, choke,
clutching our chemical masks,
and take it in, the hot mustardy, mace juice
so we know what it's like
when war ruins the air.

Everyone outside, waits by the exit door, heckling the afflicted,
waiting to see how the gas affects each Private hurrying out the chamber.

Some itch. Some cry madly. Some foam at the mouth.
Some cheer and gag. Some claw at their eyes. Some
flow uncontrollably from the nose and cack cack.
We lived. We laughed at each other's suffering. It was okay.

I fell asleep that night and felt burnt inside.
Not the CS gas.
I missed someone and didn't know whom.
I thought all of my soot and anger
would soak up someone's clean heat by now.
Who would cry if I died in a weird way?
Nobody.
All this because I thought I would look good...

A wet canvas tent has a smell that is lonely.
Soldiers are the opposite of poetry.
Drivers of death.
Death is not that different than
waiting on someone to want you.

Looking out towards the long woods,
I watch the hummingbirds, wings a-blur.
Just a blur moving them around.

I look at old photos of that boy
and I wish for a man to appear, but he is gone
and I keep gazing into those blurry photos
and wish I was better.

Louisiana VS. The Hair Club for Men

My hair quits and quits every year
and the more it quits
the less love letters I get.
It wanders
towards the silver and black
shower drain.

A lone, daddy long legs spider
slides toward the dark, like walking hair—
I wished him well,
cupped the water, and
dumped it on him.

Fuck you, creep. You can't even scream.

The worst thing I saw today
was when, at the last moment,
the crook of his leg
reached up
from the hole of the drain
trying to hang on.

Oh, God. Me too, I say.
Me too. His misery.

I turned up the water
and the sliver of leg
quietly went away.

30 miles of the state of Louisiana
erodes away
every year
and there is no sorrow
to assign to it.

Me too. Me too.

A Night Out with Jeff Koons

"Derrick, I want to hang a train from a crane.
I need 25 million dollars!"

THAT'S NOT ART, JEFF!
WE ARE FUCKING DYING OUT HERE!

"Well I think life holds the highest value. You know if you remove
a train from the tracks, all you hear is its breathing, the steam and
breathing, the puffing. Every day it would start out, like us, breathing
some, and then get up to 80 miles per hour, hanging there, and then
it would slow down, until it breathed no more. Beautiful, machine,
hanging there, out of steam. Like us."

Holy shit. That's beautiful.

"Schooled."

Fuck.

"Oh, like two trains? That's interesting."

HEY KID

Hey kid. Look. See the attractive couple stumbling from the airplane lavatory back to their seats? The man clutching his gut, pretending he was sick? The woman talking through her messed up blonde bangs all huffing across her big smeared lips? Doesn't she look like a cross between Carly Simon and the Muppet who looked like Carly Simon?

Hey kid says, "Who's Carl Simon?" Salted airplane peanuts fall from the small hands between myself and his aisle seat.

Oh, Carly Simon was a '70s woman singer who was known for singing a song about vanity and how the subject of the song was about a vain dude, and the line in the song is *I bet you think this song is about you.* But she wouldn't say who she was singing about, so everyone thinks it's a song about them. It kind of makes you feel good knowing someone wrote a song for you even if it's not nice. At least you got a song, in your own mind?

The hey kid, splitting peanuts with his little teeth, nonplussed. I am tempted to tell him that the couple wasn't sick and that they were mid-air boning and to go see which bathroom smells like a wet bag of pennies and shmutz so I don't have to use it.

I want to tell him what they were doing to see if I can explain why. I don't do it. I am envy. I am not sure why people get a kick out of love in weird places. I want to begin writing the history of award winning, slutty summers. I want it to sound American and pissed. I'd have to make it up. Eloquent and well dressed, then repulsed and outside. Bill Hicks and Tom Wolfe together at last—7 minutes in heaven. Only one comes out.

Now I wonder about Moses 'cause I am old next to this pre-teen hey kid passenger, and he is reading a cool pocket Bible, splitting more peanuts, and I say:

Hey kid. If Moses and all the Jews really survived in the desert; and let's say maybe two magic trains totaling two miles in length arrived everyday to feed them; and let's say to eat the cooked food, two more trains with four thousand tons of firewood showed up since the desert has no flammable materials; and let's say 11 million gallons of

water a day showed up for cooking and drinking, which would take
a train that was 1800 miles long; and let's say they loved this life and
did this for almost fifteen thousand days, say that sounds super crazy
or just crazy crazy?

He says, "I don't know. It was a miracle."

Do you like miracles, like believe in them now?

Hey kid teen says, "Yep. It's just more fun that way."

Exit science. Exit cynicism. Exit mystery gloss. Exit upper class
sneaky genitalia. I look out the window. Flight lends me an infinite
concern for far away little things—swimming pools are tiny,
sparkling rectangular crystals, are the things inside of salt.

I want to know even a small miracle and become brighter than space gold.

Hey kid. We, I mean scientists, just found out that gold comes from a
collapsed star called a neutron star and came here on meteors. All the
gold we have on this planet was born from the smash of dense stars
billions of years ago. If you wear gold, you wear a piece of the most
violent thing in our universe, a thing that was made in freaking outer
space. Is that a miracle?

"Sure."

Hey kid doesn't say sure like a bored Sunday dad. He says it like he
just saw the Grand Canyon one morning but works there and still
isn't sick of it.

My travel size bottle of water. The contents lifted from the sea. Into
the clouds. Into a machine to make it better. There were creatures
moving in a drop of that water. Seventeen thousand drops in a gallon.
Is that a miracle? Do those creatures need names? A man is directly
in the middle between an atom and the entire galaxy. In the way?
Exit pride.

Hey kid. When I look out this window and I think of our country, I
think of the Army and I realize that the poor are protecting us; and
I think a new law should be formed, that if war is voted for, a lottery
must be held and 51% of all senators or their children or their wives

will be asked to serve in combat arms; and we can welcome an age where there is a war where no one dies and everyone speaks as well as they can in a kind of love that ain't vain or cynical. A clear thing. A clear love. Wouldn't that be better? Wouldn't it be a miracle if we could talk and not slice each other's throats?

Hey kid says, "I don't know. I know I like riding my bike, and I really like pizza. I don't love it. You shouldn't always say love. I love my sister. She hates pizza. You can say you hate anything. You shouldn't say you love everything."

Exit over-read bloodlust. The night comes on over the landscape like glitter catching light in a widow's bonnet. We are near DC.

Hey kid. I didn't know Arlington Cemetery used to be Robert E. Lee's rose garden. Then the Union took it over and made it a gravesite. How neat to take an enemy's place of serenity and bury all your friends there.

"Is that it down there?"

Yes. I think that's it.

"Sad. My cousin Anthony died. He was a musician. I am sad because he can't make music anymore, and we all loved his music."

Loved?

"Yeah. We loved his music."

We are flying over monuments becoming lit.

Hey kid. John Wilkes Booth caught his spur in the American flag and broke his leg after temporarily murdering a mountain. Exit the absence of poetry. Exit non-magic. Exit anti-miracle stuff. I am not sure why, but the more I look out this window, the more I feel like telling the stewardess I love her and the guy behind me and the woman reading *US Weekly*.

Ma'am, I love you. Stewardess looks at me, pauses and says, *Please bring your seat back up.* I said it too softly.
Sir, I hate to interrupt the film, but I wanted to say I love you. I mumbled it.

86

Ma'am. Ma'am, I love you.
Older Woman reading mag hears me, says, *I love you too.*
That's a funny thing.
Where are you from?

Nowhere. I just wanted to say it. I felt compelled. I'd rather not talk 'cause now I feel weird.

You're fine, she says. *You're fine.*

Hey kid says, "Why did you tell those people you loved them?" I said 'cause there was no way in hell I would ever do something like that. If I did, it would be a small miracle. Kid, things are worse off everywhere else except for Switzerland, and they are bored and want graffiti and M-80s. I'm ready to try this miracle shit. I started thinking about stuff, looking down, and thinking about national stuff, and now I feel as alive as all sea lanes. It means nothing to that guy. Thanks for the uplift.

Kid says, "Thanks for telling me about Carly Simon. Should I look her up? Is she good?"

I like her music. I like that one song I guess. Crazy smile.

I look out the window and remember a teacher saying:
Never write about explicit beauty, and never use the word love outright.
Find a synonym.
And never ever ruin a compliment by tacking on the word finally.

Looking out the oval, descending like something, I see the light of the countryside. I love you. Easy. You're beautiful.
Finally.

My Voyage Accomplice

For all the support you give, I will call you girdle.
You, my singing ally, my voyage accomplice.
Streetlight dance partner, my constant casual Friday.
Bed head rocked, Pez dispensing laughing spree.

Let me coo in your bazazz.
Nothing is suddenly everything when I'm with you.
When you make me laugh, every good pair of underwear dies.
You are worth every minute shivering in the drunk tank.
They can't sell this feeling. They can't buy what we have earned.
Gold suspicion.
In a world of pop lies and the formica hard sell,
you are a breeze through a bank orchestra,
beautiful relic of manners,
jean piss bliss.

Stay with me like a mattress jingle.
I may not have your looks, but I definitely have your back.

Citrus Woman! All your light is lime-light!
Thank you for all the cell phone radiation you endured
in our late night chats. Your early death for me means a lot to me.

Your cool is so cool, oh shit, where'd all the global warming go?
You market tested better than free chocolate
and commercially appealing babies.
Tell the moon to stop sending you fan mail every night,
the jealousy brightens and is too much for sleep.

LAVA

Every coffee table, a fort
to some child
and you are amazed that
you too used to be a puddle of Thousand Island dressing
inside a ripe vagina
and then you were the size of a case of beer
and when you toddle-hugged someone you loved
so hard,
you could only reach
the tree stump of their leg
to slobber on
and they didn't shush you away.

Noise gusher.

What was wrong with young you?
How come your tongue so badly
wanted to be in every light socket?

How come your forehead
greeted every piece of cement
like an old friend?

How come your legs
weren't the synchronized model
you always wanted?

Who could love the mess?
Who could love a rig of rolling defeats?

You wanted
someone to find you like an unmapped island
and refuse to develop upon you
to *safe* you
like a full gun at night in the sticks,
to want you
like chased meat,
to alter your dark, to change your doctrine
like a church of Christ that holds its first dance.

To lift you
with a voice that overwhelms your guts when they laugh
like a mansion.

You were as misunderstood as Arkansas
and tried to summon Hawaii inside
'cause everything you loved
was stunning and distant.
Everyone looked in your eyes and saw a boy clutching a tree stump.
Yeah, yeah, yeah, your dad stuff.

Some fathers pour their money and love into cars
because they were never taught how to slow the lonely flood
so they just kept their hands moving,
building something
so they wouldn't give in to
tearing everything apart.

Some mothers look to the heavens
and sing out to the lord all day
waiting for a song to come back,
constantly looking up
so they don't have to remember
the dirt waiting for them and the ones they love,
a grief designed by the Lord.

I sing for the ones who are coming for me.
I love you out there; I love you beyond your bloodline,
the embrace of your shins,
the pillow between your legs
the spine against my chest curving like a modern tent post
as beauty becomes a covered feeling.
Come
like free weed when the cramps keep coming.
Stay
like flowers in the salt and daylight float of Oahu.

In Hawaii
the horrors of the volcanoes barfing up themselves unto themselves
and unloading their mess
into beaches of black gold reminds me of you—

a horror cooling. A rising thing.
How do I tell you how grateful I am?

There is a drawing
in black and white
of an empty field of tree stumps,
clean cuts
that someone had chain-sawed down,
and when I think of it, I cry.
I cry, not because it was drawn so well
or that beauty had slow blown its way in
like a scotch headache.

I weep because
it isn't the beauty others see first that lasts
but the beauty that someone, at some time,
catches if they wait.

The first time I looked at the drawing of the vast tree stumps,
I saw emptiness, greed, a trampling of industry, useless loss of life.
When I came back to it,
I noticed in the corner
a silhouette of one person
staring over the empty hillside
with a noose in their hand.

I couldn't help but think of you.

You have done the heaviest of things.
You have changed my plans.

OUR POISON HORSE

The horse in our field.
The black one.
Our poison horse.

Why would anyone try to poison her?
They think boys wanted the flies on her dead.
That or the boys wanted to see the skin peel.

The pesticide scar,
healing now as the jagged underline
slowly closes daily
on the mare's body,
The underlining of everything awful
about us.

       I ask you if there is anything worth saving?

You land me
a kiss so hot
the ferns die.

A grip so tight,
the blisters return and
keep you from volunteering to carry
any more coffins.

Broken fast
like an under-chucked
snowball.

Lungs rising
like Dresden
steeples.

Another kiss so hot
the butcher's meat
is ready.

You are
this coward's
drink before the bout,
a drink to help me stand
before
the bell rings
and the crowd wants blood
and the rafters spin.

Your face is leaking.
      You're the one permanent wedding.
I'm a teenage dog in the back of a truck.
I gotta jump. When will it slow down enough?

You tell me you love me,
and it unfolds my will to live.

STRANGE LIGHT

Stray Lovers Fizz

Remind me of Spain.
Let the propane
light from the barbecue
glow the back of your hair into
silhouette.

That's too close.

Now scuttle your plans,
drive to me with the radio off,
peel out in the gravel,
drive furious like a revenge trucker returning to his favorite lot lizard,
put WD 40 on the box springs and feel that sneaky lust.
I am one of your possible outcomes.
There is no One.
You can stand in front of the mirror with a camera waiting
for the love of your life to show up. See it?

Don't be Amsterdam, be Holland.
I've never been to Spain. I'm asking you to remind me of it.
Don't just be tits, be all the tits, make yourself as wanted as tits.
Don't puss out on love.

Put some ice cream in *the dead man's float*.
You're either someone's dinner or you're someone's genius,
either way doesn't matter as long as you're zizzing delicious.

Allow me to be an ocean, allow me to freeze.

I'm saying I can hold you up.

Forget all endings that demand paradise.

Your Terror is hilarious.

Scream into a road map 'til the lungs are transmission hot:

Dear Lord, is this all you got?

Yeah? That's fine.

Some giant in the sky pushes
the head of night down
into the sea
and a crown of stars bubbles
on up. Fizzle that way.

This is the feeling inside,
when you know there's fireworks,
but your head's so heavy
you can't look up.

I know this hair is a dead willow mess,
this hair is Ally Sheedy in a staged cocaine dandruff blizzard
and
these pants pretended that celibacy was valiant.
Should we see genitals when ordering bottomless mimosas?
I'm often shirtless when plastered. So many walls.

I know a vegetarian who eats horseradish
and doesn't think that's funny.

I don't get offended easily, I don't get easy enough.
I know the hard life of being a struggling writer can leave you
severely
dramatized.

Stare down the sky long enough and learn why lightning is as
jagged as us.
Try and imagine how many will adore you and learn that math is
death.
Stand at the back of punk shows,
church fog machine spectacles, poetry readings,
and wait for someone to make you catch their bouquet.

Don't be afraid. I know now I wasted much of my young life
putting up a wooden fence
around the volcano.

I know why people compare their lovers to ballrooms.I need a suit.
I'll write my own invitation.
To the greatest dance. Open your eyes.
See the slow meteor of flowers coming within reach.

OUR LONG LOW NIGHTS

1.
Sometimes when a jazz cymbal
is played with a brush—
a steady soft roll—
I hear those rainy streets,
the cars I shoved you against,
kissing you into place.
Our shirts as skin, soaked tight, pressed close, closer.
We both hate poems that mention jazz,
which is okay, because jazz hates us.
You know it does.
Can't you see it laughing at unfunny shit?
Too inside. Hoorah for the outside kinda love.
We kiss like jazz hates us.

2.
You're not scared of living,
you're not scared of love,
you're not scared of money, sex or the truth,
but there's never enough.

3.
You said life is as short and confusing as a small, angry wiener dog.
It can tell when you're afraid of it. If you open your hand towards it,
friendly
and it still snaps for blood
it is correct to punch it hard in the neck.

4.
Let's walk to the grocery store and play "Find the worst shampoo
smell."
"Find the least sexiest peanut butter name."
"Find the in-store announcement microphone
and see who can quote Biggie and Dr. Dre lyrics the longest
using manager voice."
Look at me and say, I respect your sadness but
try to not let grief be as easy as pajamas all day.

5.
In the cupboard I find corn silk powder.
When I am bored, I sprinkle some out on the floor and Bing Crosby
in my socks.
It makes me miss the warm skin on the insides of your legs. Up up
up.

6.
I found a sledgehammer next to the bed.
Someone with a sledgehammer sleeps next to me!
I rejoiced like Berlin.
We invented a game called Find Two Things to Smash.
Whoever found the most "I should've
smashed that a long time ago" thing,
doesn't have to clean up. You want me to write you a book
of these smashing sounds.
Here. That's jazz now.

7.
The kind of love that matters
walks into the World Famous Pretentious China shop
with a 2x4 and waits for the nervous
clerk to say, "…can I help you?"
Then says, "No, but I can help you."

8.
When your chest is heavy and full of colorful medals from the day,
I'll have beers and bath waiting.
If we don't have a bath, I'll find our biggest bowl and cram your dirty
ass in it.

9.
A horsewhip snaps—the sound barrier is broken. Even the laws of
nature, even us.

10.
The poetry class taught me to start strong, end strong.
I am supposed to write down the greatest thing about you,
that I could imagine about you and unpack it.

Hmm. We ordered pizza.

We told our friends we couldn't meet up 'cause of a thing.
There were cherries and bourbon sauce in the fridge.
You dragged our mattress into the living room.
Turned out all the lights.
Watched an actor try too hard.
The phone didn't ring.
The commercials were funny.
I ran my fingernails down your arm.
We forgot napkins.
We both studied the way windows make you look at them
instead of out them
when rain gives in.

Nothing was on.
Nothing is on.

WHEN NURSES COUGH

When I first heard the nurse cough
I thought; geez,
she must not be very good at her job.

I Hate You, Anis

When asked if he could change one thing in the world,
his answer wasn't any lame diatribe about One Love,
Affordable Housing or World Peace, it was,
"I would like to make bread softer."

Anis, I hate you.

When asked what his dream date would be like
he said, "I'd rather someone else go who deserves it more.
I hope it goes well, I'll be cooking a bowl of toast."

I detest you, Anis.

How is it possible that your name is one letter away from "anus"
and no one ever makes fun of that?
Everybody likes you to your face, but behind your back…
they like you even more.
WTF?!

I have odium for you, Anis.

…which I know you know means intense dislike, scholarship bitch!
I know you can only wake up when you smell cookies.
I know that when you read that "Footprints" poem before you sleep,
you often wonder if there was only one set of footprints
because Jesus and you were actually hopping with one leg each
in a burlap sack race to baby heaven.

I loathe you with all my black roasted heart, Anis.

I hate that you sound like the Snuggle fabric softener bear during
lovemaking. I hope you choke on a lego.
That no one catches onto your dance called the bubbleguts!
Bend over the anvil, Anis, and get stretched.
It's not that I super-hate you, it's that I hate that I can't make
magic wholeness like you can.

A-holeness.
I know I'll end up seeing you on America's Most Wanted…
as a victim! USA!

STRANGE HOURS IN
NEW YORK CITY

Debris.

And the night was

and then she.

Atsomecrowdedhotel.

Warm wind climbs through the balcony rails.

Knock.
Pond of blonde. Canary
yes.

Shows up tight as a bud. Suffering white and prayerless.

To get under her skirt and drown
in the radiant medicine of now.

To withdraw fantastic
into these strange hours with her
is now.

We have nothing to talk about.

"You can see ground zero from here."

Ya? I've seen it.

Her eyes do not move from mine.
I kiss her down. I kiss her closed.

It is sincere
to me.

The car she drove broke down
and I waited as she shook Long Island free from her bumper,
and I
watched the news
tell me what was dangerous.

I boiled and boiled.

The door opened, there stood:
42 love letters unreturned, 8 dildos, 15 cocks, 2 vaginas,
5 motorcycle hip holds, 3 slap fights, 1 chase via baseball bat, 112
cold beers alone,
0 roses from lovers and 0 arrangements.

                    The balcony door breezed.

One spirit was snowing.

The other was shoveling the driveway.
Museum hands digging into me,
her legs all lifejacket.

Nude and frust. Our bodies burned like wedding gowns.

I'm trying
to make you feel
geraniums. A kind
of flower you can
eat.

                Car keys and unopened wine on the dresser.

Something red
pumping fast and steady
on a machine
in her purse.

RINGLETS

Young prom ladies in loud dresses and ringlets
      mingle outside the restaurant in oversized
            men's suit jackets, their dates, smile-smoking,

            shivering, pretending not to shiver. The thing
      you said was dead is not dead. No virgin deserves
a cigarette. We should head to the emergency room

and just pop our heads in and say hello. Tell them we
      are alright so they don't think we only visit when
            things are bad. We are breathing without tubes
                      today.

            They don't make pills yet for this feeling. It's like
                finding fruit
      in the snow. I want to call down cocktails and black tire
jacks from the heavens. I want to break into something.

That kind of good. Your eyes are the kind we have all been
waiting for.
When I hear a single note sustain in a room
      with bad lighting, I think of us.

      Both of our bodies,
          shivering.

No Walls, No Go

After the soft coals of sleep
the scratching at my bedroom door returns
and the noise
clings to the head like pools of tar,
raff-raff-straff through my swampy pillows.

I used to see boars out my window.
Now the old, familiar Wolf-Fox of Sorrow,
Brimstone sifting through his smoking teeth,
blood in paws, low crawl in the grass,
he has come.

To crawl back inside me and weave himself in.
To chew out my insides and sew himself in.
The terrible sewing.

I woke up yesterday morning and
wanted to blow my brains out,
with a shotgun.
Two shells to blow my brains on the most beautiful wall,
the cleanest wall, a pool of milk waiting at the base,
the starkest white: eggshell or matte.

Spinning while exploding.
The mad spin. Walls catching me. Pink pink pink.
This so you can see what the Wolf-Fox has done
to me, has become to me.

I am fine with being the last of my name.

When I awake in our bed, hungry for these exit songs,
there is dust splitting the light.
There is that gaudy sky, all roofs on the ground,
and there are no walls for miles.

There is only rubble, settling dust, and a breeze.

You are standing there above me
with a jazz sledgehammer…exhausted.

Sexhausted. Your shirt, a creek of sweat.
Your chest shining like a Colt Peacemaker.

Your voice is cashmere and rescue.

You say,
"My dear, true love is labor.
I will not learn how to love the dead.
No walls, no go.

There is nowhere to hang a calendar.
There is nowhere for clocks.

My love is for the living."

INSTEAD OF KILLING YOURSELF

wait until
a year from now
when you say,
"Holy fuck,
I can't believe I was going to kill myself before I etcetera'd...
before I went skinny dipping in Tennessee,
made my own IPA,
tried out for a game show,
rode a camel drunk,
skydived alone,
learned to waltz with clumsy old people,
photographed electric jellyfish,
built a sailboat from all my trash,
taught someone how to read,
etc. etc. etc."

The red washing
down the bathtub
can't change the color of the sea
at all.

STRANGE LIGHT

0- Darkness.
0- Voice.
Here is the story of one man with a strange light
and tiny blisses.
The story of wild me
lost among wild you.
I wanted to be down in the obscene with you.
I wanted to come down and see it all.
To leave the black, slow sea of the heavens.
How empty and pure peace can be.
Days with no end.
Navigating celestially.
Bored to life.

I wanted to be with you.

To taste warm blue

waves of deep salt.

The council of the heavens asked me why I wanted to descend
into the territory of those
gloriously unplugged buzzards.

I told them I wanted the song of 'amazement, horrible.'
The plush rest of joy.
The sensations of a spirit mended and becoming aware.
Those living things.
To holler among the living.
To holler under the afternoon rainstorm juice.
To cheer on that ballerina tornado
who finally gets to let it all out.
To watch my house lift away
and feel better, tornado.
To feel the kiss of a drunk dog and say, "I know. I know."
To hunt God. To wash the mud from my gun
after finding him hiding in the soil.
To put his bloodied head on my wall.
To hunger in my veins for a No trophy life. No trophy love.
To succeed at floating when people urge me to sink.
To fail at hotel bed diving.

To fall for the night buzz and sudden bugs of writing,
that cheap photography.
To smell smoke nearby when I am cold.
To grieve the way I couldn't imagine grieving.
To grieve alone and feel my muscles
growing from it.

To have one choice and choose poorly.
To be thrown from the car crash and wait in the tree line,
listening to crickets
strumming for help.
To undo the face of my enemy.
To love them silently.
To aim my lung cannons for fascination and burst
into violin when I find the one.
The mouth awaiting someone versed in sparkler,
the heart singing a sustain of patient piano blood.

I want sunlight to learn me. To learn my shape.
To learn why a bomb sings just one long note
as it falls through the air.
My shape breaking the air when I fall.
Colors bursting forth of blood oranges, fog and honey?
Yes, those colors.
I am coming down there.
I am ready to wrap my future arms around it all.

I want to dance wolf-skinny under the bald moon.
The eggshell moon.
The quarter moon that looks like an Arabic shoe.
That moon. That beat up moon,
lifting higher like a balloon from a child's buttery hands.
The looming, foaming moon,
tired of being written down or dreamily discussed by poets.
I will find out why it returns and who it returns for.
Let it gleam across me. Doing its job. I can see it all.

I want to hold the face of my lover
and then watch their hair turn beautiful as they drift away.
To marvel at young unwanted boners,
that stupid bullhorn in the sweatpants singing
"...sweatpants is a bad idea after the age of 8."

To applaud the loosened old man skin,
allowing room for weakness.
To be swallowed by darkness and welcome light as the next shift.
To watch it slip away
and not know much.
To wonder about it all and know that feeling some good was good.

To marvel at the journey of impossible lovers.
To notice the trophy missing from my wall
and know that God can be found and can escape.
For all this is worthy of experience.
The experience of undoing and becoming.
My plea was for a taste. My plea was granted.
I fell to earth
and saw what Lucifer saw on his way down.
It was beautiful enough to break
even the blackest of hearts.

0- Speed.
0- Descension.
1- I was born as a small surprise of light.
Low budget Christmas tree light.
I had a heart full of volume and grizzly bear drool.
A loud little spaz. Born hollering.
I was screaming that I made it! I made it! Can't believe I made it.
I'm here on earth you huge fuckers!
Somebody Clean me up.
My Mother relieved to have the blob out of her.
Proud as a peach pie.
My Father said, "I have a suitcase full of all the things I could not be.
I can not wait to dress him in all of it."

3- Riding upon Father's shoulders, teeth closer to the sun.
5- Mother tells me that someone bright will love me,
just not as much as her.
6- Father says, Son, look at the field.
People will come to build on you or burn you out. Look at the sea.
Anchors can hold a ship in place, or hold it back. Too many anchors.
Our kitchen cupboard is full of all my lost jobs.
A house of separate beds.
When I was young,
I was afraid of the dark.

My father was tall blue grass.
I was afraid, afraid of the punishment
of the swinging belt in the dark.
I was afraid of pulling down my pants and getting the belt
the wooden spoon, the plum branch, the belt buckle
in the dark.
Not knowing when the swing was coming,
or where it would make contact,
my Father would say, "Don't you ever do that again."
Swinging with each "ever."
Fury coloring his skin in rubies.
I wonder when rage first bit his ankles and filled his Texas blood.
I wonder when it will rise in me.

I wrote to my Father last year
that I wanted to know his life—
asked him if he was dating, and how his back was.
He wrote only
"May God richly bless you…"
Ended with an ellipsis.
Grief had stolen many of his words.
I see him as a man who tried
and grew tired of the trying.
A man with bags and bags of ellipses.
I could not fit into his clothes.
I try to fill my head with Christmas.
I asked for a telescope for Christmas
when I was young
so I could see far from where I was.
A place to wait for rain
or any kind of storm.
A tornado that removes everything, me.
I hear his voice sometimes say,
"…except for you and your sister, eh…I dunno…I dunno…
may God richly bless you."

10- Rode my bike face first into the washing machine
and felt my bones come alive. Punished!
11- Started to say the word "Shit" comfortably.
14- Got the "Shit" kicked out of me for what I told the teacher was
creative dissidence.

One day, when I felt as alone as the Hawaiian Islands
I decided I didn't want to be afraid anymore.
I was getting older, lankier and felt different

like one tasty pear in a pile of pomegranates.
At school they tried to tell me:
DON'T DO ANYTHING DIFFERENT!
DON'T DO ANYTHING DANGEROUS OR FRILLY!
DON'T SEARCH TOO FAR OR YOU WILL BE BURIED!
DON'T REVEAL THAT WHICH IS SCARY!
And a few teachers cried:
But
the kids got heart

I think this kid's got heart
no no no no no
What if this kid's got heart
Let him out
no no no no
Stand up
Up straight
Straight back
Hold still
Fashion lips tight
Soften the voice,
Unhard your stare
Mind manners
Tuck your derriere
Fair skin
No muscle
Gas face
No seconds
Little boy
Little boy
Stop crying for water
Little boy little boy
Stop crying for what you are
Submissive turkey legs, you with the chicken arms,
your face looks like animal hell.
What a fashion collapse!
Someone un-perm his curly brain.
Sit up
Suck down

Back straight black nape
Clean your neck
Wash your ass
Chin up, chow down
Hold still cradle, cradle, cradle
Sit up straight
Stand like a man, we have made plans for you, huh what?
This kid is telling everyone that Jesus' blood was diet coke!
Your rough will be honed
Do not vomit light!
Don't kiss the engine when it is running
Don't draw visions of death on your final exam, whoa boy!
Don't try and out-spin our throwing knives
Don't show off, don't show on, don't Chopin! Don't Gershwin!
Don't this kid got heart?
No No No!
You listen to me turkey legs, here's the deal.
There seems to be something unnatural revving inside you.
It could be an elephant on a bicycle. We are not sure.
There is something big inside
this little puke.
It may be losing its balance,
something elaborate inside him,
something elaborate inside this little puke.
Boy says,
"…let go or be dragged, light suckers."
Maybe we send him back into the imploding zoo of the metropolis,
where he can get more lost,
commanding the street lights.
Let him scream spazzfucky unto those golden beams,
befriending the archers of death in the shadows,
doomed with the wasted and poor,
hearing the endless hums of desire,
the air filters of the workplace cooling his wild imagination.
He does have heart
and that is worth dick.
What a puke, fantastic. Hold him down. There there.

16- I tried to not break under the rickety tables of religion,
the walls of rules. My light, damp and bare.
18- Kissed a girl in a theater play. Wanted to be in every play.

22- Alone and proud of alone. Mad at lovers who locked their fingers together, sunset eyes, citrus women AND discount FLOWER SHOPS.

Later, in my twenties, I was army,
then I was lonely as museum treasure,
then I felt free in a tiny Chevy.
In the great outside, she found me.
She was wearing too many colors to be taken seriously.
She arrived like lost mail.
She didn't trust anyone barefoot.
She wasn't afraid of anything she could see.
Lonely too, but not tragic.
She was Margaret.

Margaret's heart had no crust.
Smelled like wet black cherries.
A woman born with a capacity for sunbursting.
That was my Margaret.
Hair of dirty tinsel, brown and furious at the billboards.
Her hands were branding irons and I soon became hers.
Off to the park with a flask full of anesthesia.
The snails rolled up inside their shells,
rocking back and forth against each other.
This was a glossy summer, everything was in the ooze of love.
Our hearts spread eagle and searched, thoroughly.
I had never heard the word splendor
come out of a girl's mouth before.
I heard it when she was asleep.
She told me she still saw something
flickering in me and that it was enough to keep her warm.
It was enough.
We were not star-crossed, we were horny music.
The scorn of the boring.
Dressed in classic red rose, she lived in the teeth of the matador.
The other roses dying in expensive vases.
What kind of woman draws a survival manual for the wilderness
in case it was attacked by humans?

Spiders didn't feel scary around her.
She longs for the ocean to freeze solid so we can slide to Ghana and
vanish, into cocoa and gold coast.

A falcon dives at 200 mph.
A human can run up to 27 miles per hour.
I am slow love.
I move at the speed of bad mood lighting.
She still moved towards my poverty and loved me for years.
I loved her with all my heart.
I loved her with all of everyone's heart.
I said, "I may not love you forever Margaret.
But I will try with all of my weird might
for as long as the day will allow."
Everything is supposed to die.
It does not frighten me now.

26- Lived in the mountains. I grew a beard for crumb storage.

27- Searchlights and hot cardamom, caving in to our passion.
I loved Margaret in a crazy fashion.
Our breath, shoving.
Our lips, doin' the blossom.
She is 'nervous-marvelous.'
She was porn for dead girls.
She was a refrigerator full of synthetic blood when you need it all.
Will you fade Margaret? Like a magazine left in the window?
I can not unlace you from my head.
Margaret gave her days to me and we bloomed into bright years.
How we bloomed.

38- And so the poem and the narrator have reached age 38. The
narrator is worried about moving forward with the poem because the
next stanza is 39, and over there a little further is 40, and if the poem
continues, the poem will end. All of her light ceasing. She would say,
"Soon we will all be dust and poorly lit photography, so let's get
dumb.
You think too much."

39- Joy. Spent all our money on dumb stuff and launched it off the
roof, laughing like crows.
41- We never married. We should have. I should have. I could
never say why.
44- I blew out my back at work. I tried painting. I was terrible. I
became terrible.

48- We parted. I miss her. I beat the feeling into the walls.
My father's left hook. I'm glad she left, for her sake.
49- God has richly blessed me…

51- I dunno.

57- I dunno.

68- I dunno.

72- As an older man,
I have a dream about walking backwards through devastation,
a familiar destroyed place,
realizing at the end of the poem that I did it.
I could see things growing
once the soil had been tilled by my explosions.
There were signs littered about, some said No Loitering On This
Planet.
Some said—
No proof for all you felt.
No baster to soak in your sorrow.
No finger twitch after you've been declared dead.
No soft metal ballad at your wake.
No yellowing in the eyes to prove you stared down the sun.
No sissy strut to the throne.
No love letters rolled, lit and dragged.
No shoes repaired from running nowhere.
No burning fire escape make out.
No wedding march that was a black motorcade.
No fever kiss in every dream anymore.
No rosy easy funeral and dance party as requested.
No brawl for her once she cries resolute and leaves.
No reason to hold your fingernails in your teeth and wait.
No staying power for things caught in the wind current.
No binocular peep show and wishing for the neighbor's life.
No day nakedness courage.
No lust laid upon you like your favorite jacket found.
No cloud cover Sunday bliss hand in hand.
No shade in the desert.
No anchors for battered vessels.
No black smokers below birthing new land.
No signs of the end.

No signs on this road.
No good end, No lovely road.
No markings on the road for a grand return.

I'm 49
The night is coming, the great night, falling slow and easy.

I'm 57
The wind moves toward me like a coffin on a luggage carousel.
I'm 68
The dark is possible, the dark is always possible.
People falling in it everyday.
Margaret's passing hit me like poison,
like I had been drinking it all my life and finally let it work.

I'm 72
I am tired and fading.
49
57
68
72…

73- I cannot die. I will myself more life. I must keep
writing myself down. It's how I don't die.
No pine tar heart!
No costume armor parade!
No graceful widow's walk!
No sissy strut emergency room,
No hard star glimmer in my eye posing as starlight.
No white light dream sequence.
Fuck you. Death. Fuck you.
No sequin sorrow shining from within me, giving up.
Hurrah Hurrah these ghosty places.
Hurrah Hurrah these places I have walked upon and who have
walked upon me.
Hurrah Hurrah the drunk calligraphy of two bodies
still unfurling in my mind.
Margaret, Margaret. My luminous Margaret.
Margaret, your nervous laughter feels like home.
I sing of your sudden lust,
your smashed glamour, broken chest
custodian, golden memory thief,

your ease in finding the things I lost around the house,
my keys, my phone, my heart, my glasses—
things I could never retrieve.
Every mansion in this coming town is bored, Margaret.
Every mansion in heaven.
All their closets full of shiny skeletons. Worthless pearls.
They will never play our music. Never.
The angel of death early to your cocktail party. Early is always worse
than late.
Fuck you Death!
I must keep you alive in my head Margaret.
I loved your full résumé.
I loved your throaty kiss.
I am gushing.
I am ready to fill this night with senseless acts of
ha cha cha, no retreat, no quarter. I am dumb!
I'm going berserker.
I ain't goin' west
like the sunsets of death.

I am still in your tornado ballet. Still longing to feel you lift me away.
Hurrah Hurrah your shadow that finds rest inside the black of me.
Hurrah Hurrah the fight, the unwinnable fight that seems winnable
when your legs are locked around my hips, doubling me.
Hurrah Hurrah us loyal dogs.
Hurrah Hurrah the echo that is not forever.
Hurrah Hurrah the things that do not last.

Hurrah Hurrah the night, the naked, and the poor
floating upon it, that gloss black boat.
I will not let my story be held hostage.
I want it to be haunted.
I want another chance to flow in through the windows
like a Baptist miracle flood. 10 more minutes!
I could not will this poem into life.
This is what it wanted to say to you.
I am sorry in six dead languages.

The no poetry of I am sorry,
the lost volumes of I am sorry.
This is all of it, Margaret.
I am sorry for wanting what I was
and I know you are sorry for wanting that too.

I let too much hell burn my choice for us away.
I tried to blow the black of my chest out
with a flashlight.
Your arms, even when apart, wrapping me bulletproof.

Is this you? Coming to me?
Your light, my beacon, the river shining a way out.
The tar pits of night are sucking me in.
All hail the ships
that sail beyond dusk
without wind.
All love is love in the dark.
All love is love in the dark.

I fought wrong. How I loved writing you down.
Now. I am coming home.

When we die
it is poetry
that leaves the body…

Derrick Brown's Famous Last Words

Do I just swallow it, or do I have to bite down to kill it?

So are you a hippie or would this be considered drifter sex?

Is that all the wasabi you got back there?

Would it be alright if I joined the gang, just for the summer?

THE LAST WEATHERMAN

The weatherman lives a life of no poetry.

"Science holds no imagination to beauty.
Science is all that is real."

He performs his final run-through before the regular evening taping,
muttering the phrases: "Partial Clouds…Hail among thunderstorms…
High pressure system…a pusssssh of energy moves into the region…"

His life is control.
His life is a table for one, always able to find a seat at the movies.
Tandem bikes make him vomit. Someone is always pulling
someone's weight.

His desk at work is dominated by "the small dogs in big shirts" cal-
endar and a dumb coffee cup.

At home, there are no plants. Why take care of something that tries
to die if you ignore it?
His kitchen is just a place to stand sometimes. Someone he doesn't
know sent him a package so he didn't open it. It feels like a book.
"No thanks." His bed has one pillow. No one believes it but the
weatherman is as happy
…as he is.

Something peculiar happened during the regular evening taping.

"And…speed."

"And we're back now with Derrick Brown and our AccuWeather
Forecast, what's going on out there in those wild skies of ours?"

"I'm glad you asked Lea because we have some heavy tzz bundling up
to do this weekend due to another high pressure sister…pushing its
way like a frag-tzzzlgrp freak caboose…full of PCP. Precipi…PCP.
Sorry. I'll pickup…and rolling…A strong thunderstrum of brain and
blzzz blaze of hell, pure hail, hell falling to the refreshed, is there har-
bor for the forgotten…tzzzglpn forecast-in, cave in…Hail, my will,
my tzzz cave…tllzzzgnp. Hup. Can I retake that? The whole thing?"

That was the day it started. The day his words fought their way out
of his mouth.

He walks to work every morning. The sky is only blue.
The clouds are there.
The coffee is just hot.

He looks at the picture of someone he once knew on his desk.
The day the words took over was the first day he noticed anything
small.
The picture used to tell him, "I don't need you to be love, I need you
to be a solution."
Something strange happened.
He noticed his coffee mug for the first time.
The smooth handle.
The stains on the inside lip.
The dumb 'coffee makes me poop' slogan.
He never thought it was beautiful before today, but he started to
think about beautiful holding devices and his mind began to exhale,
after a full life of inhaling.

A homeless man outside the studio asks him
what the weather is going to be like.
"If ya get a chance, tune in. We need more viewers."

He plays a broken toy piano. Old green cut off military gloves. Today
the homeless man says,
*"Give me some insight brother. I gotta find shelter tonight or what?? Don't tell
me to tune in or I'll eat your mouth."*

The weatherman tried to summon a sensible response
but all that came out was,
"Well, thunderstrums, a blaze of hell.
I don't know what tzzz going on!"

He said, *"Holy moly. It found you!"*

"What found me?"

*"The bad weather of words, buttnugger. You needed it too.
You a big ugly vase and all ya flowers is dead.
The bad weather of words commands us to celebrate and spin away from cynic-blood.*

124

Consider the battered piñata.
They may beat you to bits, but there's still some good candy inside. Gobbledy.
You just got to shake it around.
Notice the living. Bzzrp. You need to spaz-bonfire.
The bad weather of words tells you to burn like Watts,
before the riots, when the fire was building inside people first—
Is a hard brain gonna fall?"

"Yes."

"I'll find shelter. Gloompschlzrp. When I get too wet,
I have to go home and change. Enjoy the burn, freak caboose!"

It was the day words found him,
His lips were like wet 9-volt batteries.
His lungs shrank and ballooned and his breathing turtled and grew
as his heart rose away from its old scuttled shell.
He watched his break room ice cream melt, as it should, but now, it
was not a mess, it was officially a chance to lick his hand.

The weatherman tried to warm up
for the Saturday evening taping. It all came out as:

(1) There is going to be a tasty solid chill in the air, frost on the
ground tonight so let's do the penguin belly glide down some bas-
tard's hill.

(2) The oncoming humidity is going to unbutton every denim blouse
and unzip every costume.

(3) Set your windshield wipers to gospel high yi yi!

(4) The wind is so calm you will want to whisper back 'I missed you'
in fake French. Lefondle. Du swoosh ette.

(5) We have a stampede of storms on radar. I shall ride it for nine
seconds! Suck it Luke Perry!
It was exhausting, but Saturday night finally ended
the way the weatherman had secretly wished it would,
like a good poem—unexpected, a warm quiet.
It ended like moonlight into the ground.

So here's to punching holes in the ceiling and waiting for the stars to suck. Here's to the bad weather of words finding you, to the nails in the black air being pulled out by the passionate claw hammer, the night sky blanketing down upon us in jet black silk and octopus ink.

Here's to the thunderstrums and your oncoming blaze of hell.

"If you are cooking something in the kitchen tonight,
slow down and see the meal in the pot.
Notice the pot.
Maybe leave the meal in the sauce longer.
Look out the window.
A high pressure sister is definitely coming our way."

THE COMPANY MACHINE

SHE: Why won't you come to church with us? I have a bible for you. They're going to be talking about heaven and miracles.

YOU: Can we just imagine at some point in my life I realize that I have dirty clothes.

Everyone comes to a point where they realize they have dirty clothes, mine finally comes, the smell has finally gotten to me and only when I start to smell it can I decide to get my clothes clean.

If you call the company for me, I don't get to enroll in the benefits of their membership program. So time passes, and I am tired of the smell, so I call The Company. The Company tells me I can get rid of the smell, but I must get my clothes washed in The Company's washing machine.

I order it. It shows up and it is not assembled.
It is wonky and confusing.
Much of it seems to have been designed at a time when we thought stars were lamps and the world was flat and you had to kill something to say you were sorry.

I am confused and instructed over the phone to go to a local company office to have a man in a strange suit show me how to disassemble it and then reassemble it so that the washing machine works correctly for me. Each company store interprets the manual differently. I chose the company office with the sauciest looking employees. They were cool, but they kept telling me to just feel it in my heart and I'll have it running in no time.

I decide to read the accompanying instruction manual to figure it all out for myself.
Some passages in the instructions are beautifully written and some are parables on how to assemble
the washing machine.

I JUST WANT TO GET MY CLOTHES CLEAN!
WHY NOT SAY, JUST DO *THIS* AND YOU WILL SEE *THIS*!

The first half of the manual tells me how the boss is angry and jealous and the second half of the manual says how the boss of the company sends a piece of himself, the nice and poor people loving side of himself, to teach everyone how to assemble these washing machines. He mentions that his employees make mistakes. He also mentions that his employees wrote the manual that he tried to dictate.

I try all day but I can't put this machine together with poetry. I decide that I do want clean clothes and I will wash them in the sink from now on, my way. So, thank you, but no I don't want to learn about heaven or resurrection from anyone as confused as me. Confusion is convincing when fused with conviction.

SHE: Does everything in this life have to be so black and white?

YOU: Yes and no.

THE NIGHT: Shoot. Resurrection once? I come back all the time.

SCANDALABRA

MEATLOAF

My Mother is washing the dishes and singing
a song about someone dancing on the moon.

She stops to pat the globe of her stomach.
"So full."

I help her with the dirty meatloaf dishes and pass them from the table.
The gunk slides through the soap
and the green goo slips across her strong hands.

There is a flash of light every time she turns her palm through the soap.

My Mother has a small diamond
that she received on her wedding day.

It was given to her by my Father,
as a symbol.

It was very affordable.

I always asked her why a diamond meant
that you loved someone?

Why not a brick, snail or wombat skull?
Why not give someone a pair of fuzzy handcuffs
to show the world that this creep will be with you forever?
Why not a cat's brain to show them you are crazy about them,
as long as they keep feeding you and leaving you be?

There is dishwashing liquid in a brigade of bulging bubbles
and the 'tink spink' of moving plates and my Mother is singing
again.

To her, the diamond ring was a cheap but special reminder:
My Mother says when she first saw the ring
it caught a light that shot into her eye like fresh grapefruit.
She says my sister and I did that too.

The filthy forks sifted through her hands as the disposal burled:
"Gnrlwygnlrygnlrywy."

She stops singing and turns off the disposal.
Her face turns the color of the kitchen sink.

Water off.
She tosses through the plates.
She pulls out a rubber doodad to check the garbage disposal,
continues this for about ten minutes.

I wait for her to say it.
I can feel my face, ready to burst like a cloud.

"It's gone. I can't believe we were just talking about it and it's gone."
She patted my head and handed me a paper towel.

"It's okay Mom. It's just a thing."

"Not really." She starts to weep a little. "Excuse me."

She goes to the bathroom to blow her nose,
returning, kisses my head and goes back to washing the dishes
with me,
scanning every bubble's gleam for the rock.

I roll my damp paper towel into a ring shape and give it to her.
"If we weren't blood, I'd marry you. And I'd stick around."
She replies, "That is sweet. Illegal, a little weird,
but so sweet Derrick."
She grabs some tape so it would stay wrapped up.

I sneak outside to the neighbors' place
and steal her a brick
from their garden.

When I come back in,
She laughs at her jackass son
and begins to sing that song
of someone somewhere
dancing on the moon,
a song about a boy spinning in the dark
with a beam of light.

COTTON IN THE AIR

Your polished back is arched like Saint Louis.

I can see your fingers pushing into the bricks
when I lift your hair
to smell October drain from your neck.

You are cotton caught in the air
I unfurl all the tight laces in your body.

I move on you steady like a fleet of ships pushing ice.
I want to break it all.

Your tank-top strap slips down the huh huh of your shoulder
and I will not strain meaning from this.

I am waltzing a wrecking ball.

Wading in the dark felt Tijuana paintings of your hair.

Molting my bed clothes / uncoiling towards Sahara.

All I want to do is hot lust you into dead sweat.
To watch your legs, those bent sickles,
to watch them shake
like poisoned wrens.

I am gnashed and dazzled.
Smother me in the exhausted thrust of your yes...
wet
as all exploding laundromats.

Rough and shuck, throne-sucked, enter the tongue-dozer.

May I be the image you turn to
when you are heaving alone,
burning like Halloween in Detroit?

I am breathing up your legsssssspitting at the hiding nightingale.

Drift your boobies into my mouth
as a held back Shakespeare might say
and I will be that doped up, spinning Victrola.

La la la la lala.

I want to make love to you while you're wearing figure skates
until the hardwood floors are toothpicks.
I want to kiss your throat in a dressing room with my hands
bound around the slow song of your voice.

I don't care if you made that dress, hippie.
I will shred it until you look deserted. You are island.

You're as restless as a New Orleans graveyard in a storm
with all your coffins boiling up to the surface.

That's all this writing is.
You are across from me and the soup is cooking.

I sit up all night listening to your dental records.

Let's research exorcisms and screw the hell out of each other.
I will carry your steam in my mouth and tell everyone I'm haunted.

Daydreaming of the evening of loud struggle.
Call my name—I will cascade like a suicide.
I will fall upon you like a box of fluorescent bulbs
dropped from a five-story building.

I will do anything you ask...
unless I have been drinking,
then it is opposite day.

I can't believe you can sleep through all this.

Chunks of brick in your fingernails.
Mortar on your pillow
A bomb shelter
sketched on your skirt.

Safe.

PATIENCE

I can not love you until you can love our beautiful waitress
in the simple way that I do.

Valentine's Day in Dreseden

I feel as ridiculous as faith based food,
directionless as piss in outer space
when you reach for me.

Our love would be as dumb
as a bomb on a boomerang.

Figs in your lips.
Let's not fall in love.
I am tired of stroking that kitty.

Don't come to me all dressed up
in a peanut butter and nightmare sandwich
wondering if I'll bite.
Your eyes as boring as a desert photograph,
your body, a nude model for bad hotel art.

I know your type. Wingdings!
Zapf Dingbats! Verdana…wide!

You're a European mess
rolling around in my favorite dress—
a mouth full of hell
and a chest full of hell yes.

Big deal, your eyes are green and gray.
Shut off the night vision, creep.

You kissed me on the throat.
What is wrong with you!
That's where I make my money!

Our sex is going to be like throwing pasta against the wall
to see if we're done. Drink casual tea.

Speak love all you want.

I don't believe what you say
but
I appreciate your tone.

THE HEALER

CHAPTER 1

At some point in the vanishing history of a couple, their home fades from a place of shelter to a museum of what once was.

There are no new photos in the frames.
The picture light above the painting of Avalon is busted;
the island is timeless in a constant Pacific twilight.
A medical degree yellows in an old English font.
The front door looks locked but doesn't lock.
The carpet smells like El Paso.
The cobweb motels on the ceiling corners have been vacated.
The trophies have become what all trophies become.
A typewriter is frozen and lost.

A young couple, but disease has made their home smell convalescent and dank. An ashtray is flooded with cremated nerves from nights turned rubber and long.

CHAPTER 2

Years ago, they picked up a widow's Steinway at an auction; it is the only artifact in the house that has ever been dusted. The scent of lemon wax and oil wafts from the oak of its hammered black gown. The piano lid stays open, always, and a Polaroid of Margaret's face rests there. The picture shows a wild softness in the mouth and something else in her cheekbones. It sits on the tray where the music is supposed to be read. He never thought music was something you should have to read.

Dr. Steve Timmerman is a fine pediatric doctor and a failed pianist. "My dad used to tell me at recitals; every decent man fails at something that he wanted more than anything." He sits at the keys like a hunter in a deer outpost, waiting for melody to sneak by so he can pin it down under his fingers. As Margaret lies in the next room, coughing up colors, he kills the keys through the California evening. With every wrong note, he is reminded of how much he misses the smoke of her voice.

His interest in progressing as a musician deteriorated long ago, when his obsession with obtaining a medical degree took hold. Since high school, he imagined that a successful career was connected to a successful love life. His parents were broke, miserable and slept in separate beds. His plan paid off when he met Margaret at Columbia University. She had a problem with burping out loud in the library. He offered to pat her back and weaseled his way into a first date by sliding his request in between the many technical benefits of a good burp. Since then, he has never wanted to leave her side.

Eight years of marriage saw its share of difficult times. It would be unfair not to mention that these times were often overpowered and blurred by an honest fascination and admiration for each other. They never knew love as a mad affair with sex on subways and the claw marks of jealousy. They had a steady love and slow evenings. A perfect night usually consisted of a pizza and some craft, like when they made paper airplanes for Tobias, her nephew.

Margaret couldn't make a normal paper airplane. It was never a normal anything. Margaret's paper airplanes always had atomic banana missiles, turrets in non-aerodynamic places, secret refueling areas and at least one escape pod.

Steve loved Margaret's creativity and tried to chase it with logic.

"I think you should call it an escape hatch, honey.
Boys know the difference between escape hatch and escape pod."

Margaret steels her focus on the X-Acto knife. "Thank you NASA, but I know the difference and I am making the escape pod so it can go down the escape hatch."

"What's the tinfoil for?"

"That's a fire proof love letter launcher that won't burn up when it passes the sun or when satellite lasers try to take it out 'cause it looks like a foreign probe. It's very handy when the pod gets lost in orbit without communication. I dunno…just standard issue stuff."

She would get lost in a project, and he would soon be lost in her, staring at her intense relationship with just a piece of paper, his crap plane with its popsicle stick refueling rod and sturdy wings still parked on the desk's tarmac.

He remembers how she cussed when she sliced her finger.
He remembers fetching her a band-aid that night. In the morning the bed was covered in blood.

CHAPTER 3

Steve had dove deep into the study and experimentations on cell research related to von Willebrand's disease. Margaret started experiencing the symptoms of the disorder about two years ago.

All the grant applications had been submitted.
They were ignored.
There are more people mating with horses than people carrying her disease.
Who cares?
Normally, not even him.
He poured over medical journals like a dumpster diver.
Margaret had become bed ridden.
She was always cold.
He noticed blankets in department stores now.
His colleagues knew she had between one and six months to live.
No one could tell him to his face.

Steve tried to set up small fundraisers, but Margaret shot every concept down.

"Honey, I think your effort and your attention to me has been so sweet. But to be honest, I feel too guilty. Don't you remember watching those celebrities on television hosting those tear-jerking telethons for…I dunno…MS or cancer, but probably wouldn't give a shit about it if they hadn't contracted it themselves so—"

Steve jumped in, "This isn't a congratulatory thing so we can pat ourselves on the back. So many people love you—the kids in your class, family, everyone. I am only suggesting that we have the vision or…grace to accept their help. I could do so much more if I could just get some funding. If research persists, research prevails."

"I know the point you're trying to make and I know that your motives are out of…ya' know…I know they're pure. But it's us, ya' know? The world shouldn't care about Margaret Timmerman's poor blood clotting any more than they should care about your bad golf swing—too many problems out there."

The doctor stared at his terrible carpet full of coffee stains and blood. "My golf swing kicks ass and you know it." He love, loved her.

CHAPTER 4

He bathed her pudgy body. It was so badly bruised, she couldn't stand to have the shower water strike the back of her legs. He could only barely touch her skin due to the spreading of the sores. He missed sex only when he bathed her. He imagined the moans that emanated from the pain in her limbs to be the moans of something more erotic.

"I think you're beautiful."

She moved the soap slowly across her stomach. "Oh sure, with my white face and my hair falling out and the purple skin and black blotches. I wish I knew this was your taste back when I was shaving my legs and plucking my eyebrows. I look dead."

"You don't. Margo, I really like your big nose and I like squeezing your hand. I like noticing the cracks and the little line things about it. When I squeeze it, I feel something good shoot through my body. It's weird. You do look better. A few more bruises"

She leaned forward toward the faucet. Her face had flashed into somberness. "I look better? I feel so much worse. Steve. I just want it to be over. I'm not kidding. The pain is...This is so..."
Her tears dropped into the bath. Concentric circles spun towards the porcelain walls.

He leaned over the clouded bathwater as the bubbles crackled. "I was going to tell you that there are some new theories about the medicines you've been taking."

"I don't want any more medicine. I don't want people to send any more cards saying they're praying for me. I don't want anything. Prayer isn't working. Medicine isn't working."

Steve's brow crunched. "Just give me time. I can't tell you how shitty I feel about being a doctor and having all these connections and still not being able to do anything for you. I can't stop trying."

Margaret's wet and stringy hair tilted back. "I'm not supposed to be fighting this, honey. I don't know how you have this unrealistic hope. I don't think you would if you knew how I felt. What do I have, a week? Two weeks? I am tired and I think…I'm just done."

Steve released a shot of hot water between her legs.

"If you kill yourself, I'll sue you."

He kissed her forehead and whispered something else in her ear.
She stared into the murk.
Her hand moved through the soap bubbles like a razor through snow.

CHAPTER 5

It was 1:26 in the morning when Steve arrived at the UCI student research labs. It was here, on a steady diet of black coffee and poptarts, where he had spent every free hour attempting various combinations of chemical reactions to create a medicine that would cause platelets to clot quickly for those with her condition.

He decided against telling her in case his theories were wrong.

Only two Danish doctors had come close to a cure and Steve had sussed them for all their documents, lab evidence and recent findings. Then, he made a discovery of his own. One of the rats infected with the disease had significant clotting after being treated with a crushed pill form that rushes blood and platelets to a wound or scar. The only problem was that the acceleration of the clotting was much quicker than a human's normal response to clotting. Doctor Timmerman needed a person to try his formula on.

Tomorrow, he would put an anonymous ad in the paper for volunteers and hope that money would come to pay them after the trial was over. Whether it was junkies, homeless people or students, it wouldn't matter to him. Time was running out.

Before he turned out the lights to the lab, Dr. Timmerman caught a glimpse of the stainless metal tray in front of him and the small pile of pills. He knew that he ethically couldn't give a possibly lethal dose of medicine under the auspices of a clinical trial. He could feel frustration curdle in his fingernails. He was stuck.

He quickly lifted a scalpel to his forearm and made a one and a half inch incision. The blood globbed onto the cold formica. He was exhausted from the countless hours of testing that it seemed to hurt less. It still smarted like a son-of-a-bitch, just a little less.
He placed half of the gray pill on his tongue and let it dissolve, felt it slip into his gums and under his tongue.

Five minutes later, his lungs reacted first. It felt like a good dose of oxygen was pushing its way out. Gripping the wound on his arm, he waited. He thought about Margaret in that tub hours earlier—the one with the lion's paws at the bottom—and how she always made a prune comment whenever she got out and he remembered how he loved that.

His senses were sparkling.
He noticed everything about his body:
The turning in his stomach from forgetting to eat.
The cold feeling between his socks and skin.
The wet, hot sear on his forearm.
The creaking in the bones of his shoulders.
A desperate gurgling down by his liver.
And then exhaustion.

He fell asleep with his hands in front of him, as if playing a piano in the air.

CHAPTER 6

Two hours later, Steve awoke with drool cooling his cheek. The wound had almost completely healed. His eyes widened as if he were a kid watching miracles on TV. He thought to himself, "My God, I only took half a dose." He felt like a dart had lodged in his neck from passing out on the desk.

He thought, "What does this mean? What could this mean?" He went to call one of his colleagues, a friend from Dartmouth. As he reached for the phone, he noticed that three of his fingers, between pinky and thumb, were slightly sealed together, on each hand. "What the…?" As he forced his sealed fingers apart, blood emerged.

He looked around the table for glue that he might have dropped his hand across while sleeping but there was none. The skin between each digit had grafted to itself.

As he drove to their home from the lab, Dr. Timmerman kept turning up the FM radio a couple more notches every few minutes. He wondered if he was losing signal and saw that the volume was now maxed out. It took forty minutes for him to realize that the holes of his ears were also slowly healing.

CHAPTER 7

It was 6:45 in the morning, and the light on the highway was breaking across the lanes reflectors. He called his wife.

"Margaret," His voice thumped dull in his head as if in a thick plastic drum. "Something has happened. I might need you to help me. Oh, and I might need some of your nail polish remover and eardrops. I'll be home in like twenty. I can't talk now. I'll explain later. Sorry for waking you. I love you."

She might have said something, but it was hard for him to hear. He hoped she had answered the phone.

CHAPTER 8

Steve could feel his heartbeat increase rapidly. The insides of his arms felt like Japanese rice. His lips became chapped in the corners and stretched. He stumbled up to the garage, removed his shoe and tore his sock from his skin. Bits of black cloth had infused with the flesh. His toes were becoming one lump and it threw his balance out of whack.

Wondering whom to call for help he stumbled into the kitchen, but then realized he still wouldn't be able to hear if anyone was answering. His pores were stretching and this cold burning sensation caused him to cry like he was lost in a department store. He scratched a note with a marker in big block letters.

Steve sat down at the piano, while Margaret slept nude in the next room. With the knuckle of his right hand he pressed a D note, then a G, then an A. He waited. He felt the piano vibrate under the knobs of his hands, but he could only hear the shifting and growing pulse of skin inside his skull, like diving into the deep end. The slow sobbing broke the skin on the sides of his mouth and his lips were now bleeding.

He saw himself in the black reflection of the piano lid and watched as the blood in the corners of his mouth quickly morphed into flesh.
Red, then pink, then white, then pink, then beige.
His eyelids ached like they were made of nickel.
Steve gently pried one eyelid open with the side of his thumb.
He could see the photo of Margaret, frozen on the piano, resting there like one page of a great, short symphony. He stared at it and knew it would be the last time. His thoughts poured out like notes: "You were mine. You were my life and beautiful and unlucky. You were music. You were my music."

He went to the cupboard and struggled to crush up two-dozen sleeping pills. He placed them in a glass of water and then stepped into the room where she slept. Steve placed the glass and the note on her nightstand beside her unfinished crossword puzzles. He fought to breathe through a narrow passage in his nostril, pushing out air like a thoroughbred.

He saw the shadow of her hips in the gray light. He gently pressed his mouth to her neck. He wanted to kiss her, but could only bump against her tender skin. His mouth was now fully sealed.

Screams of agony were muted in his chest as he removed his clothes.

He lifted the sheets that smelled of her favorite fabric softener. She lay there on her side, heavy in sleep. He pressed his body to hers, then gently grasped her hand for the last time. He felt warm and terrified. He tried to relax. In the morning she would find the note and the glass. The note had just two sentences. "I will see you soon." That was the first. The second sentence, written frenetic and fumbling, seemed to hold an entire species' misery in the tiniest bit of space: "I tried."

As he pressed closer to her, the skin above his eyes began to seal over.
He moved the sticky bubble gums of his hands to the thigh of his woman...
He was glad they were alone there, in that room.
The curtains held back the sunrise.
The alarm clock remained silent.
Unsalvageable bodies.
He knew that soon, they would be one.

Days later, a coroner will approach.
Removing his mask outside the rancid home,
he will remove a cigarette and imagine the conversation
a mortician will have with their families,
gently and tastefully suggesting one tombstone,
one grave,
and one casket.

THE RETURN OF CHRIST

Trying to let go of you
is like trying to spit out my teeth
before the dashboard
roars into my throat.

Something lonely in the air sieves through the screen door.

I want her to be warm on this ship, arms full of cake,
shaped like a broken white viola.

Here come the songs of divers,
falling into quiet.

The creaking of aluminum masts
sounds like someone walking away, slowly.

If Christians can wait this long for their savior to return
on an unknown open-ended invite of prose,
I can wait a few years for my beautiful figurehead
to soar from the prow of another's ship.

The night turns to cold coffee.
Channel 16 is for distress signals only
and I listen until the night gives up
on being endless.

FULL METAL NECKLACES
for Andrea Gibson

You are laughing up moths
and bleeding in your boy pants,
breathing your poems out like burning garlands.

Soon,
a woman from the audience,
full of woe and strange posture is crying on you.

Your hands sheath themselves
into your back pockets.
You're not sure what to say.

I don't know what kind of advice
can make the anchors in her neck
go away.

Your arms wrap around her
as if someone is going to steal her skin.

You hang there
like a constellation settling in the black,
a woman slung around your neck,
snot and tears
staining your boring sweatshirt.

You speak for a living
because you hear the dying.

Hang from chin up bars to lengthen your arms.
So many to embrace.

We are necklaces dipped in your voice-box, shining metal struggle,
crazed and heavy.

Your sweatshirt—a travelling canvas,
painted in the unfurling mess
of us.

POWER

For a reason,
it is hard to clean up blood
when it spills.

It stains with permanence,
even the underside of our skin.
It tags the spot we were wounded in,
the size of the tag tells the size of the wound.

Maybe this is why, at the Rainbow Motel in Memphis,
they had to use a cut-off saw to break away
the large reddened concrete balcony piece
that Dr. King
breathed his spirit out on.

Top

A soldier once told me "Killing kills your sense of seeing the living as sacred.
Once you get that out of the way, you're not afraid to die
or make others do the same."

War is just one side losing less.

Master Sergeant JC and I write back and forth.
We went to the same basic training, Airborne school
and were stationed in the same Airborne battery.
I got out from the 82nd and he stayed in to run the whole battalion,
fifteen years later. A huge, buff man with a laugh like a side of beef.
He is now guarding highway 8 in Baghdad.
He has been advancing rapidly in the ranks.
I used to call him Sarge,
Then Smoke,
Now Top.

He told me about a meeting with his younger sergeants
after the troops had been walking through Kut.
They kept getting pot shots at them. Zing. Zip.
The Sergeants told him it was slaughter
to go in there without armored personnel carriers.

He relayed this info to get gear before the patrols
and the Captain relayed his orders back:
Patrols in Kut must continue on foot according to Centcom.

I started to ramble about the frustrations of Military inefficiency.
There is a difference between talking to someone about war
and talking to someone in war about it.

"Don't do it, Derrick."
Do what?
"Don't make me feel like we're dying for nothing."
I won't. You aren't, They aren't.
"We are freeing these people."
Right.

"If we didn't do it, no one would've"
I know…

"I miss my wife, Derrick"
I talked to her. Cindy is good. The dogs are good.
"I miss BBQ and Sam Adams."
Cant help ya there.
"So when can we fire at will
and have the soft targets off the list
and are engageable
Mosques, all that."
Soon.

Where am I, John?
Cannoneer #2, Round loader, Breech puller,
Foxhole digger, Non-rigger, Fuse counter,
Aiming pole runner, M60 toting,
ambush crushing Grenadier, Specialist Brown is now
just a writer, far from the noise. I am proud of you.
I want you to remember home.

The bars are full of laughter.
The ribs are falling off the bone.
Summer is coming.
You can golf in the twilight.
I want you to miss these things.
I don't care who wins.
I want you to stay alive.
Keep your weapon clean.
Stay alert.
Stay alive.
Kill everything.
Fight everything.
Just stay alive, John.
Keep yourself alive.
There are prayers in your boots.
March.

Come home awake.

I will tell you a story.
This is the job of poets.

Staying alive is the job of good soldiers.
And the dead are better soldiers.

This is not how the world needs you,
The world doesn't need any more sudden dead.
Even though you're good at it,
War
is just one side losing less.

Beyond The Clearing,
A Sounder of Boars

Through the curtains of night oak,
into the clearing near the back of my house,
the sounder of boars returned.

Snouts along the ground
swaying like metal detectors.
Tusks, white as shards of new soap.
They advance, steadily
creeping with blood stains on their chin fur,
plague in their hot breath
surging slowly to my yard.

Tuskless sows grunt in cadence
as piglets swing their heads agreeing with the noise.
Stripes in their bristles emerge from the tree line
and soon in formation, they advance.

Hooves of the sounder crunch
through flakes of autumn like the boots
of a new search party.
I am surrounded.

They do this every year, in the same season.
At first I wondered if it was a friendly ritual…
they growled their mystery.
They waited in silence sending up rough grunts
and guttural howls, bellowing an awful melody,
haunting the mist.

As their black bodies filled my field, I became scared.
I wanted to kill them.
I do not love killing animals
as much as I love having killed for food.
The meal is tastier than the hunt
for certain men.

At first I appeased them with acorns and candied pecans.
The third year, I moved on to confrontation.

I kept some spears in the coat closet behind the vacuum.
No gun. I drink too much to keep one near me when I begin to sink.
Some days I am bloated passionate.
Some days I am a brick in a pond.
The gun would be a bad, loud joke.

When the long tooth boar began its mournful song,
I launched an attack.

The remaining spears were weak shots.
My arms trembled from lack of nutrients.

I launched the spears as fast as I could, from my porch,
lobbing them in an arc for distance.
I scattered those bloody bristles.

They returned in an hour
and the army of boars waited.

I did not know what they were waiting for.
- a meal?
- my home?
- blood?
- me?

Another year and I moved to giving them sacrifices.
Small turtles and a wristwatch placed in the clearing.
A box of photographs.
They would attack them in a rage,
but only when the God of the boars
moved his hoof, tapping it onto the ground.

The rage and shredding,
The movements of vicious instinct and wild dread.
There wasn't much more I wanted to offer them.
The few objects I did own were precious to me.

I offered rabbit last year.
They dragged it from my porch,
impaled in the leader's tusks
blood streaking my wooden planks.

I watched from the window
as the beasts ravaged it, charging into each other like drugged rams
warring for the remnants of its body.

Sliding back beyond the clearing,
they marked my land with the hare's tragic red mess,
leaving the bits of its carcass to rot.

This year was different.
They came and posed.
I turned on a floodlight.
Some were red as demons. Some were black as Georgia molasses.
Some were glossed in sweat. Some tusks were three feet long,
swooped towards the pocked moon.

I held fast in my house for days.
A hostage to the beasts.
The infant boars eager for something and yelping.
The God of the boars
standing in the center
while the others formed a disciplined circle.

I was running out of food.

The last of my tack was a half-skinned deer, a small buck
from the summer crossbow hunt.
I kept it in the garage freezer.

I carried its dead weight to the porch
as an offering and wished I had a phone
or a big wife who could wrestle animals
or neighbors with the gumption to check up on you
or friends with guns.

I stood there behind the dead buck, desperate, alone,
caked in bits of ice and defrosting animal,
skinny as the spears in the field.

I displayed the young meat for them.
The boars grunted and only the God boar stirred,
lifting his evil neck and holding his ground.

They all remained staring into me
with marbleized black olive eyes.
None approached.
I was exhausted.

"What do you want from me?"

Nothing.

"Do you want me to come with you?"

The long God boar surrounded by the others
patted a hoof at the ground.
They rose and spread like the red sea, a path to the God boar.

"Can I pack my things?"

The red boar snorted goop onto the soil.

"Can I write a letter?"

The God boar squatted onto his belly
and the others followed as dominos.

I came back inside to tell whoever find this:

I don't know if you should look for me.

If you do, I couldn't take any of my posessions.

I am probably beyond the clearing
through the oak
deep into the thick, lawless wild
owning nothing,
wandering
in a most beautiful ending.

GROCERY LIST

Be more forgiving.
Substitute goodbye for I like your face.
Spend two nights a week not drinking to forget.
Listen to your body.
Listen to someone else's body.
Get limber.
Don't dog yourself to feel humble. It never works.
Lift others up onto your back until you are sore.
Write for yourself a movie that doesn't end.
Eat a churro slowly.
Kiss your mother on the cheek and don't miss.
Remember that now is barely now. It will soon be back then. Stop.
Don't text anyone while talking with anyone.
It will morph you into an asshole.
Finish Everything.
Get Milk.

Church of The Broken Axe Handle

for Buddy Wakefield

Lord, my friend's heart has disassembled.
So broken, it is red dust.
His pen is rust.
His body is not a house built for silent prayer.
It is a church of blood, raw and razor pumping
for that scar power, axe handle snap and dirt face gospel.

We belong to the same church.

Our clergy: blacksmiths and cut throats,
former party murderers
and never again to be bound choir.

Our lobby holds a bowl of holy water
filled with terrified jellyfish.
Come wash your hands in it again.
Feel the frenzied sting of his creatures.
It is the Lord's idea for us to feel the sting.

Our Lord is the Lord of the moray eel incisors.
The Lord of the whale carcass murders, Hyena brutality
and sharks glossing towards blood.
The Lord of the vampire bat swamp bones
and crocodile gut stomp.
The Lord of the Possum army moving their evil eyes through the
twilight.
The tearing, the tearing. The nourishment.

We are the horror in the Lord's love poem.

He has given birth to us to sing in the fight.
We are the organ full of bees, enemies of silence.
Sing out your death rattle constant.
Sing out your questions with the force and mess of dynamite stew.
Listen for an answer echoing,
spinning warmth inside you like a Leslie speaker.

You will hear it when you are so alone.
I know you are alone and soaking in it
like solitude was blood
and the night is the letting.

Your heart races with the pressure
of everyone in the room
finding a slow dance partner
but you.

Tap in. Tap the shoulder.
Love is yours. Make the first move.
Lose the ones who stepped on your shoes.
Love is yours.
Let it be its horrible self. Learn it.

Our church is fully armed. Return to it with devotion.

Your spirit is a ready gun. Load it yourself.
Only fire it into the worthy.

Rise above the grief bait and sugars of sorrow,
spin searing gold from all that copper noise.
You are better than the demons whispering in your cheeks.

Lift us into your belief, let it blast.
Let it be a bloodbath
with your innards on the floor,
no apologies.

Welcome yourself back to ugly glory you.

This is not typical church.

We welcome you, you new crawling psalms,
you drunk choirs
you gouged melodies
you nasty bags of glowing mercy.
We welcome those with unpaid bone tariffs
those raised by the missing,
those boys who got lost in the eyes of another boy
those who loved the cities that hated them

those who keep putting on their gloves for boxing the sanity out
those who couldn't scratch their golden tickets because their nails
were ground down from clawing their own way
out of their father's casket
those who couldn't get skinny enough to get to the front of the line,
those who couldn't stand anymore so they built splints out of words,
out of their own words.
Depth charges yes!
The choir charging the audience
with tambourines shaking the hell from their teeth, yes!
Kick me when I'm up, yes!
Hallelujah we are fucked! Yes!
Bring it on so we can prove the strength that will lift ourselves out of
the magpie swamp.
The worst thing you have ever been through is always a fair fight.

Come to the church of the new.
A building that only says lost and in bold letters, found.

This is not typical church.
This is a low attended funeral,
a piñata full of doves that demands
beautiful release…

Buddy, You are church.
Open the gates, my friend. Send St. Peter home.
All are welcome.
Turn on the golden lights.
Guide us in.
Someone you have been waiting for is coming.
Guard your heart minimally. Security threat, beige.
You can carry a knife and still trust everyone.

Carry it in your mouth.
Every time you open it,
we await the sharpening noise of worship.

Cry out into the darkness
the sermon that doesn't cease:
You can not be abandoned—
you can only be released.

The Long, Outstanding Saltation Into Wild Open Air

OKLAHOMA CITY, OKLAHOMA

I stopped at Galileo's bar in the Paseo district.
Free beer if you are featuring your poems.
Someone tried to sell me dirty DVDs in the parking lot.
One was called ass ass ass where the phrase triple ass would do.
He didn't want to trade a poetry book for the movie.
Poetry will be worth more than lo-fi fake lust soon.
I remember making out once with a woman
in a handicap elevator around here.
Rowdy stumble-touch
is better than classy balance.
The night air here is flat.
The day is crème and crimson.
I know Dylan Thomas left a beer can onstage when he spoke at OU.
It was on display for years.
Someone stole that empty beer can.
Did they put it up to their ears like a seashell?
Middle American exit noise and dust bowl wrath poems.
Not worth more than
hand streaks
all over an elevator wall.

NORMAN, OKLAHOMA

My friends Beau and Jody are getting married today.
I got ordained online and agreed to pastor their
wedding in the middle
of this cross country tour.
He has a lumberjack's beard and a strong Springsteen half sober face
like a gunstock.
She has a white tinsel smile and jar of black olives for hair.
I remember a Father, slow dancing with his daughter.
Clumsy, gentle and unashamed.
He held her like he would miss her terribly.
When he let her go
it was true and perfect.

162

TULSA, OKLAHOMA

The moms here sure are attractive.

PORTLAND, OREGON

You screwed a lovely blonde woman in the street.
She said, "what if a car comes?"
You thought, then that car is a pervert.

ANCHORAGE, ALASKA

Even the glaciers look desperate and royal.
Everyone here misses someone.
Come here if you are in love with
how things used to be.
You can feel far, even with friends around you.
A town becomes a gorgeous warning for shelter
when you realize that if you pass out
in a gutter,
you will be dead frozen by morning.

COEUR d'ALENE, NORTH IDAHO

The cliffs lift sharp and green from the water like soldiers' shoulders.
The patches of snow rest on the lake like a coke mirror.
Not much happens here
on purpose.
A house sits on the lakeshore with a woman fishing from the dock.
I hope the fella inside knows what he has.

SHOSHONI, WYOMING

Pass the mellow hush of Powell
and all the curving river gorges of Thermopolis
to get to Shoshoni. The town is a sad song.
Don't you love them?
The Silver Sage bar smelled like stuffed raccoons and mop water.

She was as kind and busy cleaning
for most of the town was dust.
I feel at rest here. I feel this town settling in my mouth.
Across the street of abandoned shops,
someone spray painted a poem next to a drawing of Geronimo.
Beautiful words
and no one to read them.

BOULDER, COLORADO

Lori Lee was a sweet kind of skinny,
tan, flowing wheat hair.
She was spilling with Shakespeare.
He sure knew how to kill someone off.
Everyone in Boulder looked like a fitness coach on whip its
or a gay hiking instructor.
Where are the gay bars?
We both didn't have much to say.
Paul Newman had just died.
The snow crunches loud when you stroll and say nothing.
Some people shouldn't die.

DENVER, COLORADO

The Mercury Café is an artisan chocolate éclair, dark, sweet and full
of weird goo.
At some point during the show,
I threw some chairs to get at an audience member texting.
It's an awful way to sell books.
There sure are a lot of folks here with piercings.
They look like fish
that fought hard
and broke away from the line.

OMAHA, NEBRASKA

It says the good life,
but it feels like the aftermath of Goliath's belly flop.
We met up with the fellas of Delta Spirit at a venue downtown

and danced our demons out.
You don't have to have beautiful
surroundings
to be surrounded by beauty.

CHICAGO, ILLINOIS

Their bones are bright
and full with freezer burn.
The bicycles are drunk.
The lips of Chicago wrap around me in sausage skin.
The city is a heaving castle with asthma, rising from a lake that
doesn't end.
Shoulders full of concrete and black ice, lift me up, lift me up.
Heaven's pub. Speak easy to me.
You laugh so hard in Chicago
your ribs rip and it feels like you're kissing
a dark haired woman
in a river full of brats.
Best people in the whole damn world.
18 degrees and still BBQ'ing.

DAYTON, OHIO

The Wright brothers are singing in the wind.
The university is full of black beauties.
Everyone gets lost in Ohio.
I dropped my virginity around here at 19 and
it reminds me that I want to tell my friend
who has a broken heart,
"Don't ruin love
by wanting it so bad."

TRAVERSE CITY, MICHIGAN

Come see the opera house dance floor where I split my pants
at the world's most gorgeous place for a poetry show!
Come see Michael Moore's sweat garden
and beautiful theater of cheap popcorn and starlit ceiling!

Come see the cherries placed into every object known to man!
Come watch the world blossom in a secret code.
Do not chop down the Cherry Trees.
Lie about it if you do.
Come prowl the stillness.
Come see the lake as it calls to the lovers
and come see the lovers answer
by walking into it, hand in hand
and never returning.

DETROIT, MICHIGAN

I used to see Detroit as a place that burns.
Detroit has pockets and they are filling with the machines of art.
You gotta let something burn to the ground
to build something new.

PROVIDENCE, RHODE ISLAND

There were so many pretty girls here
I just went to bed.

BANGOR, MAINE

At the haunted Bangor Motor Inn, Cristin rang up my room:
"I'm gonna murder you!"
Then she hung up.
I soon called her back. I said,
"You're gonna be dead!"
She responded, "That's not right.
We're all gonna be dead. Work the verbs. Try again."

ROYALTON, VERMONT

We showed up to Mongo's ranch house in a tiny van
and we were covered in hot exhaust and cramps.
There was cold beer waiting and it wasn't bug season.
When you really want beer and it is already waiting for you

like a Northern war bride, all cold and horny?
Vermont is the sweetest secret that should only be shared
when you have pancakes, cold beer
and orange-red-razmatazz trees chucking its tickertape
in its annual parade of maple privacy. Skeeters!

JAMAICA PLAIN, MASSACHUSSETS

There is a little white house aptly named The White House
full of musicians, artists and writers that puts on shows.
I spent the day at the huge pond, rowing a boat with some friends.
The swans swam in pairs, showing off.
JP licks and so do I!
I met a woman on the street while I was carrying my laundry.
She was a belly dancer. Weird how that happens.
You got a big burden
of smelly clothes
and someone offers to help you.
We chatted about wine, staying limber and
other things I know little about.
We didn't get it on, but I sure felt good in her place.
The sepia tone show at the white house was in a little family room.
Perfect, no amp and packed.
There is a bag of chips with a retractable string in the living room.
You can pull it down from the chandelier
and offer it to someone and as they reach for it, laugh as it zips
back to its home.
I too want someone to tug on me with the smell of ocean
so I can zip back home.

WHITE RIVER JUNCTION, VERMONT

This is one of my favorite towns in the world.
It is about as big as a slice of bologna.
Everyone here is bundled up and smart.
I need to open up a bar here.
Maybe it can be a library too. This town demands secret passages!
I can't read when I'm tipsy
but maybe I can find a secret passage and somebody can read to me.

HANOVER, NEW HAMPSHIRE

The leaves are changing like teak in the sunshine.
The students are wishing for warmth and it doesn't come.
The dorms are kissing chambers trembling in brains and bad sandals.
There is a bridge that makes you feel
like you are flying into green laundry.
I could live here
if I was allowed to teach
all the things I am still trying to learn.

WEST LEBANON, NEW HAMPSHIRE

If you stop at the Four Aces Biker bar,
you should get a bunch of breakfast.
If locals are looking at you,
they are just waiting for you to
introduce yourself.

COLLEGE PARK, MARYLAND

Kenton, Gabi, Harry,
you are all I know of the good of this city
and you're from everywhere.
The stromboli is as big as your brave-guts.
Write your way back home.
Drinking and talking about the worst things we've ever done.
Julie was kind and too thoughtful to make that game forgettable.
Heather was doing push ups.
I think she was getting ready for Armageddon,
her arms, sleek as solid snakes.

NASHVILLE, TENNESSEE

In a drawl,
I missed you.

FRANKLIN, TENNESSEE

There is a garden here
where over 1000 civil war soldiers died
in hand to hand combat.
You can touch your fingers to the bullets embedded in the brick.
This is also a town known for having a large population
of contemporary Christian musicians.
So much carnage.

CONWAY, ARKANSAS

I remember a fight almost broke out at the pizza diner.
A dude from Texarkana who came with a female reporter
kept saying odd things, he was tired of liberals and faggots.
He was talking with Buddy.
Buddy is gay. He doesn't look gay to most folks.
Buddy is very buff.
Buddy was not afraid and offered to set him straight.
"Tell your family you got bowed down by a faggot."
The drunk dude and the kind reporter left before paying.
I think she was crying and I felt awful for her.
I felt great for Buddy. His eyes as wide as the Mississippi.
We found out later that the reporter
dropped the dude off with a few quarters at the gas station
100 miles from Texarkana and told him to find his own ride home.
She said he wouldn't stop yapping.
I didn't know her and I was so proud,
I had to write her down.

ARLINGTON, TEXAS

The waitress at the Cracker Barrel restaurant
thought we were in a band.
We told her we were writers and she gushed about her son
who was also an artist and made hip hop beats.
I can't remember his name,
but I remember her glowing like a bowl of halos
when she spoke her son's name.

AUSTIN, TEXAS

There are clearly two lands called Texas.
There is the land of my Father, in Cleveland, Humble, and Houston.
It is a land where you could blow up a car
and no one would care.
It is a land where we chased goats
and got chased by hornets and snapping turtles.
It is a hard land to be raised on and I see it in my Father's laugh lines.
Then there is Austin.
Prettiest women in the world: a liberal town with zero snootiness.
You can fall in love with someone, but for only four years.
Then, they graduate, leave and it is all understood suffering.
I remember drinking with the mayor once at a poetry show
and felt like the town had figured out endearment.
My father came to Austin to see the show,
ragged from the drive from Humble.
A woman was talking to him for too long so he got up
mid-conversation, kissed her on the cheek
and walked to smoke one of his Salem cigarettes.
I thought that was a great way to excuse yourself.
I know he loves people, but maybe he isn't used to them.
I see myself in him as he stands alone at the back of the venue
watching me, watching himself.

AMARILLO, TEXAS

There were wild horses.
There was your friend who just had a child.
Amarillo is where wind and babies meet
so the children dress like kites, grow up and usually lift away.
At the Nat Ballroom, you can dance on the same stage that
Buddy Holly got hoarse on.
The road never ends. There is love in the barren.
The horizon is a train in quicksand.
We sold body tackles for a dollar.
This meant I would tackle you for a dollar.
We needed gas money. We were moving on.
Wild horses stomp and my spirit falls in love
with being alone.

TRUTH OR CONSEQUENCES, NEW MEXICO

Near the Rio Grande, we pulled over at night.
The sky, gashed with stars,
only the high beams of truckers scooting beneath it.
Anis joked that this is what he usually saw during love making.
It was so dark,
he ended up picking up a souvenir rock. He called it his lucky rock.
I saw that he lifted it from the spot
I peed in when I got out of the van.
I wonder if he kept it?
I wonder if I should tell him? Nah.

HATCH, NEW MEXICO

Blood red chilies hung on the doors as year long wreaths.
It is 93 degrees here on Oct 26.
We ate at Sparky's BBQ.
Michelle stood behind the counter,
beautiful and far away, moving in the kitchen
like a youth pastor's wife.
It has been the same lemonade recipe for ten years.
The moose above our table seemed to be smiling.
I would like my head mounted with a confused
look on my face, looking back at the person I thought I knew,
now bringing me down for petty cash.
The sausage and ribs are glazed in secrets and butte powder.
The lemonade and you, they are your father's pride, Michelle.
Michelle, please get in the van.
The river is drying up.
The world awaits your teeth, your joy illumination.

TUCSON, ARIZONA

There was a train moving behind the stage door,
every 15 minutes.
I wanted to open the backstage door
to just get on and go.
The people in the audience would have never
forgotten that show. Especially if I was chopped up.

LONG BEACH, CALIFORNIA

The Prospector
Alex's bar
The Queen Mary's observation bar
Joe Jost's
The Dirty Bird, (Crow)
The Pike
The V room
The Red Room
If you can hit all these places in one day
then you win the tournament of champions.
Tough to win because each place seduces you.
These are the places that put out the blaze.
Long Beach, I will be your unknown gutter laureate of 4th street.
I will sing from the Gondolas of Naples
to the Merchant Marine staring out from Ocean St.
He is waiting for the brothers who didn't make it to shore.
Long Beach, you are opening your arms.
Bring us your graduated broke, your sheared babes and floor peanuts,
your booze parade of labor, your renovated bones,
your shipyard ghost war.
You are spectacle in the sea of blue collars,
a gala of people hanging on
in unison.

VENICE BEACH, CALIFORNIA

There is a small butterfly park
and the butterflies left the park to follow me,
zig-zagging as guide-ons down the sidewalk.
The nature
of mutual delight.
A crazed looking man
got off his bike
to sing to a few pots of flowers.
Crazy has its dividends.
Great day in the history of great days.

RENO, NEVADA

All you kids
left to rot here
are brighter
than all these casinos
smashed together.

DONNER LAKE, CALIFORNIA

We jumped in.
You shouldn't. Ever.
You will perish with a horrible look on your face.
Ice is supposed to be frozen.
This lake was a former harlot:
Beautiful on the outside
and ready to kill you
if you ever tried
to stay inside
her.

SAN RAFAEL, CALIFORNIA

We invited the entire audience onto the stage.
They did. We were all the show. We are.

BERKELEY, CALIFORNIA

Bringing poetry to Berkeley
is like bringing a turkey
to a turkey farmer's house
for Thanksgiving.
Thank God that the farmer still tells you
that your turkey is the kind
she has been waiting for.

COTTAGE GROVE, OREGON

I spent three nights here recording a poetry album,
at Richard Swift's house,
sleeping behind the controls.
I asked the brilliant fuzzy head of Richard
if he knew where he would hang his hat,
his final resting place.
He said "Here, in Cottage Grove. We love it.
So many people come here and don't want to leave.
You start to love the rain."
Some souls never know
where they will plop down.
I envy those who can do the math.
The rain comes down, slow enough to see it somersault.
The Ax and Fiddle has good beer on tap
waiting for us as we stroll damp and ready for the night.
There is a small theater doing a play about a robot.
What more do you need?

BELLINGHAM, WASHINGTON

It is the last stop before Canada.
We sang songs at breakfast.
We sang songs at The Beaver.
A new president was elected tonight.
People ran through the streets with American flags.
Most of them artsy looking types.
I wonder if all those flags were just waiting in their closets
like their favorite coat,
and everyone
all at once
was overwhelmed
with the welcome feeling
of new snow.

I Love You Is Back

Debbie

Attached to a little red plane,
A sky banner floats
above.
DEBBIE, DO YOU LOVE ME?
Not, Debbie, I love you.
Not, Debbie Jenkins Specifically, you're beautiful.
Not, Debbie, will you marry me?

It detached from the back of the little red plane,
The banner whisping down the sky.

I wondered who it would land on.

I imagine that person having a hell of a day
if their name happens to also be Debbie.
I could see it making her believe in God.

ALL DISTORTION, ALL THE TIME

Someone plug my lungs back into the guitar amps!
I want to live
on all distortion, all the time.
More over-drive!
Aren't you sick of being appraised as just wholesale?
Aren't you sick of sailing on listing ships?
Aren't you weary from playing cellos with ex-lover's bones?

I am.

I want a piano that will not warp outdoors
when the rain demands slow dancing.

I want to skew the difference between Tai Chi and Chai tea,
and end up drinking a tall glass of your graceful force.
I want to lick my hands after I touch someone that has just become
razzle dazzled by the huh?
I want birds to come close enough to hear them speak
Aviation Spanish.
Abierto, abierto.

I want your criminal record collection in my throat,
and my thumb in the electric ass of this all night jukebox.
I want my shoulder blades mounted
in the museum of the most fantastic knives.
I want church in a bar and a bar in every church.
I want to pass out and hear you say Amen with your body.
I want a skeleton night light in the closet.
I want your wow in my now so we become NWOW.

I want free shit to not cost anything.
I want to feel like a disco ball of fish hooks
so you can hang on my words, how we spin in small miracles of light.

I want my kitchen to be a Brazilian dance floor
with a pot of your sweat in the oven
and a fridge stocked with booty lust.
I want new sheets. Guess why?
I want your silver muscles cut into a quilt.

Let me sleep under your strength.
I want more pony lamps. No reason. Just give me the lamps.
I want to sing this into all tail pipes until I'm exhausted of puns.

I want to smell the everything.
I want to remember that the sky is so gorgeously large,
I feel stranded beneath it.
When I gasp beneath it,
I only want to gasp
for more.

ONWARD INTO THE ZIPPERS OF DAYLIGHT

When I run, I move beautifully
like a chandelier in a hail storm.

Leave your horrors
before the numbness travels to your legs.

Loyalty is nerdy. Loyalty is possible. Loyalty is all.

We are lovely, strong and ugly.
When the lights are out we are but wrinkles and noises.

She leans into my light and melts my candles:
"You are mathematically elegant.
You are mathematically elegant squared.
Wake up. I think I love you."

I think sounds more true than *I do*.

This dumb kite flies towards your lightning.

Woman Sleeping In a Room Full of Hummingbirds

Teased by success.
We're like vampires in a tampon factory.

The only good monologue has mistakes.
Mistakes make honey interesting.
Silly putty, ice cream cones and chocolate chip cookies
are all accidents. Me too!

Hush hush pants, my legs carry me out to the twilight poison.
That means nothing! I'm spread.

I didn't have a grasp of what was happening to my heart
until after the first break up. I was plowing anything
that smelled disinfected and didn't wear pookah shells.

I started making lists to get the stripes back on the tiger.
I was watching my stripes slip from my spine,
laying there on the ground like a bunch of parentheses.

Go away therapy. Flush home pills. Make lists.
My lists started out strange.

#1. Do something rebellious to get out of your comfort zone.
Try graffiti.

My first graffiti art said, "Don't pierce your babies' ears.
They don't like it and no one thinks it's cute except for you
and your friends with jet skis." This was coming from me,
the only boy
            who enjoyed getting circumcised.
#2. Write something down that is impossible and write it as possible.
It took me a while but I came up with this little gem.

"Be on time. Ride time like a suede cowgirl. Break it.
Make it sack out, then canter. Trim its hooves.
Run it into the ground. Oh no. You just wrote about time! You are
one of thoooose horrible people!"

There was a whole bunch I made, which are a bit embarrassing, but the last one became my favorite.

#46. One day, when you are tired of being broken
and in the city,
carefully strap little LED lights to hummingbirds,
at least 52 of them
and release the birds in your lover's bedroom at night.

When he or she asks what is going on
tell them to be still,
lie there all broken and impressed,
and yes, only kids make wishes.

Watch her mouth move,
astounded at your invention.
Watch how it turns your lover young
with each awe of shooting light.

See your lover as young. Do not kiss them. You will now go to jail.

Wish your burdens upon those birds.
The birds can take it.

Go play.

CRAWLING TO THE CHORUS

Everyone on the television is laughing
at the black boy comedy.

His growth stunted by prescribed drugs,
he plays an adopted son.

I remember being nine and wanting the boy to come to my house,
to make me laugh as hard as the people in the studio audience.

I wanted to be part of a great washing body of laughter.
I wanted to know why they were laughing and if it was real.
If it was, I wanted to be there.

I wondered about the lucky black boy's life of laughter.

I wondered if he hated being small.

While his show ran that night
and the fan mail poured in and the money dripped down
and his family met at a Champagne fortress for the airing party,
my mother was bleeding profusely during episode 3 season 2.
I felt too small to help.

My father, hurling glass at her chest.

I always saw blood as Halloween syrup until that moment.
I wondered if it was real.
Them both screaming for demons to come out of the other.
Trying to anoint each other with oil.
Their voices escalating into the wood paneling.

I curled up in the bathroom as chrysalis.
His hands pummeling like a turbine,
her hands sewing at the air,
their voices soaring like fists full of swans.
My father moving his hot ballet across her.

I could hear the neighbors closing their windows
when I finally stumbled past my sister,
who locked herself in the bathroom.

I heard their vows crawl back into the bible.

My Father sinking like a battle ship into the couch. Panting.
My Mother told me to sneak the checkbook from the kitchen and I did.

My sister and I crawled and tried to hold our breath.
My Mother sharpened into a strength she had never known before
that evening when she decided to steal our car to somewhere safe.

We piled in the garaged Datsun and
when it wouldn't start we became
      terrified.
Three more tries and it finally turned over.
My Father opened the bedroom door to the garage.
I can see him standing there with the anger gone from his eyes.

The car finally started
and it felt like reverse would never come,
and when it came,
there was no relief.

My Father just stared at us for a moment
and pressed the garage door button calmly.
We drove away forever.

I wondered if the black boy wondered about nights like this;
revolving around his celebrity
as the audience takes to the sound stage,
knowing that his job is relief,
delivering a joke someone else wrote for him.
The audience rises in laughter
like a chorus
I always dream of joining.

Eating the Hull

A man in Texas and I discussed our most favorite
feeling we can remember.
I think I mentioned a kite and some wine at Catalina
or a sailboat dinner.

I asked him about the greatest feeling he could remember.

He talked about a time
when he worked at a sandwich shop in Amarillo and had to make the
          condiments
and on Fridays he would fill a surgical glove
with guacamole
and slide his hand in it when no one was looking,
opening and closing his fist through the green thickness.

He made an Ooh Ahh Oooh Ahh sound.

I asked him if he ever got lonely.

He said, "Never."

Recording Textbooks For the Blind

I had never gone inside the blind man's house before.
I had read his graduate text books
on Astronomy, Polynesian music theory
and strange mathematics into a tape recorder.
All mumbled for him for five bucks an hour in Flagstaff.
I thought it would be nice to work from home and help someone.

It dragged on me.

After two hours of recording
I would begin skipping things that seemed unimportant...to me.
I also added jokes about various pictures in the book.
"And this is a picture of a naked lady with an abacus. What's that
doing in here, and when did scientific calculators get that big?"
I never told him that I skipped some stuff.

He couriered a message to me to bring a 40 watt light bulb
and that I would be reimbursed
during my next tape delivery.
When I arrived he asked me to help him replace it
so he wouldn't get shocked.
After a few seconds,
I wondered why I was replacing a light bulb in his house.
He said he could tell a difference.
The place seemed cozy and well decorated.
I asked him if it felt like home.
He said nowhere felt like home.

I asked him the most pedestrian of questions, "What's it like?"

"Oh, living alone?"

It's not what I meant but I listened.
He said when you are alone you drink slower.
He said he had a bottle made of bone
and how different it felt on his lips
compared to ceramic.
He says when he speaks now, more often he means what he says.

Of course, I wanted to know about living with blindness.
I wanted to tell him I wrote a story about a time
 when I was an Easter bunny for some blind kids,
as if that would make us feel bonded.

He mentioned that all he has ever learned about stars rolling in gas,
the sound of Hawaii
and various algorithms
come to his brain as my voice.
He said I was in his head and that when I spoke,
he expected a load of random
information.
I kept moving my hand near him, gently.
I kept trying to tell if he could tell that I was looking at him.
Standing there at his door I tried to tell him
how cold I was because I wasn't wearing a jacket.
I must've sounded nervous.
His record player was dusty.
I didn't know if I should tell him.

I asked him one night,
dropping off the cassette, what he dreamt about.
He said each word crisply:

"Shapes.
Mostly shapes.
And a woman.

How are the light bulbs doing?"

How Did I Become a Damned Cartoon?

It sounded like a good idea at the time. Helping kids, right? Helping blind kids on Easter looks good on paper. My buddy Buzzy said to me, "We're doing this benefit day for the blind children's center of Orange County. We need someone to be the bunny. You like kids, how they can be louder than a pile of Hawaiian shirts, how they poop for fun. It's for a good cause. Why not give it a shot?"

If someone ever asks you to be in a bunny suit for blind children, I recommend that you don't do it. Someone is gonna get hurt. In the face. And it will be a small Mexican child.

I should've realized that most of these kids would be picnicking outdoors with food smashed all over their blind faces. Luckily Easter this year fell on a smoldering weekend and I was the dope cooking in the furry suit. I was so soaked in sweat, I thought my underwear was crying.

I could hardly see out the huge rabbit head.

But there I was in 90 degree heat with a basket full of eggs in a suit made of carpet and lead trying to trick kids who had never seen a rabbit into thinking I was a rabbit that is as tall as a human and has bad taste in multi-colored vests. And why would I wear a vest with no pants to a child's party? I'm going to send a letter to Winnie the Pooh.

At the park, I struggled to leave my friend's VW bug and finally we walked holding hands to the picnic tables full of kids. The Easter Bunny is supposed to be a dude and I doubt he holds hands with anyone in his sad egg shaped home. Buzzy yelled out: "Hey everybody, the Easter Bunny is here!"

Silence. No reaction. Not one yelp.

Buzzy whispered to me, "Oh man, we got deaf and blind kids. You're gonna have to really turn it up a notch. If they get restless, just give 'em some more candy and that should keep 'em busy."

A woman walked up to Buzzy and said

"Hey Buzz. Thank you guys so much for coming. This means a lot to us. These groups of kids have been blind since birth. You'll have to explain to them what an Easter Bunny actually is. I'm sure they'll love you."

Buzzy confidently nodded at her; "I think it would be better if the Easter Bunny explained himself to the kids, one on one." I spun my constantly erect ears toward him. I tried to wipe the sweat from my forehead, but actually ended up wiping the rabbit's furry head with my glove. I cleared my throat.

"Hey kids. My name is...the Easter Bunny." One kid lifted his head up towards me but did not look at me. "Your name is the Easter Bunny?"

"What? Yes. I am the Easter Bunny...and my name is the Easter Bunny. I am...a rabbit...who can talk. It is Easter so I've brought you all some eggs. Some...are painted. Some have toys or sweets in the eggs...that I squatted and gave birth to. I'm a dude."

Buzzy elbowed me on that one. He then guided me to a bench and gathered the un-amused children around me. I don't know how well they could hear me in that muffled suit.

"Is this a jacket? This feels like a jacket or a rug for the bathroom," said one of the eight-year-olds as he ran his hands down the front of my costume.

"Are you here 'cause of Jesus?" asked a smaller kid. "Aren't we all?" I replied.

An older kid piped up, "No. I'm not here 'cause of Jesus. I'm here 'cause um my Mommy and Daddy made me. Jesus didn't make me. Jesus only saved me from hell."

"I know. Would you like an egg with a jellybean in it?"

Now all these hands were all over me as one of my paws instinctually moved to protect my rabbit breasts. They were asking questions one on top of the other and weren't waiting for me to respond:

"Why are you wearing that?"

"Can I have more candy?"

"Are you supposed to be a dog or a monster?"
I interrupted to get their hands off of me. "Hey you guys want to play helicopter? Follow me."

I hopped off toward an open area wondering if any of these kids actually wanted to play in this heat. Three kids tried to run and follow me. One ran into a metal garbage can, which always sounds worse than it feels. One girl got clothes lined by a badminton net, which I found rude to set up in the first place. One lone, six-year-old Mexican kid named Miguel made it to me. He stuck his arms out and just put one hand on me, just to make sure I wasn't going away. As volunteers tended to the injured, I asked the kid,

"Would you mind if I took off my headpiece, just for a little bit. Would that freak you out? I'm really burning up in here."

"What headpiece?" said Miguel.

"I'm wearing this rabbit costume and I have this mask on and it sucks. I don't think anyone cares or thinks I'm actually a rabbit, I don't think anyone knows what Easter has to do with bunnies and plastic eggs, the Catholic church and druids, so if you wouldn't mind, I'd at least like to take off the mask for a bit. I'm seriously cooking in this bitch."

The kid looked off toward the street. "Sure. I don't care. I just want someone to play with. We can be friends today."

I grabbed the sweet little bud's hands with my paws and began to spin him in a circle until his legs lifted up into the air. With his arms outstretched and spinning faster, Miguel actually squealed a little.

"Heeee. I'm flying. I'm flying. The rabbit is making me fly! Look at me everybody. Look at me! I feel like I'm flying."

The saddest looking kid of the bunch was laughing his head off. I felt good. I felt like a good person. So that's what it's like. All of a sudden I felt un-ridiculous. All the pain that this volunteering had led to had become worth it. I gave some kids some jellybeans and made a few kids laugh. There is something for me to learn from every person's story.

I thought maybe, if my life is built on suffering a little bit every day so... And then my paw-gloves slipped off my sweaty hands and Miguel went flying across the grass until he landed in a spread eagle belly flop by the sprinklers!

He ended up getting the wind knocked out of him hard. Miguel lifted his little wet grassy face up, crying.

I stared at him, frozen, like I broke him. They took him into the shade and I waited for him to stop weeping.

Buzzy explained to the workers what happened. "Are you O.K. Miguel? I am so, so, so sorry."

"It's O.K. Easter Bunny. I would like to do it again, but my ribs hurt too much. Oh, goodies." It was his version of cussing.

"You're a tough guy Miguel. I would like to give you my mask, so you remember me."

Buzzy whispered in my ear, "You can't. It's a rental."

"Miguel, I would like to give you this colorful basket. You can put things in it. A basket is a thing you can put things in, like a bucket, like a funny bucket."

"Thank you Easter Bunny. I will put things in it, maybe today it will be a hot dog."

Miguel gave me a hug, told me that God would make him alright and that I was sweaty. He said he couldn't wait for me to come back. I told him that next time he loses a tooth, I would sneak into his bedroom and beat that tooth fairy down with my lucky feet and then we could play a game where no one gets hurt by Easter, everyone wins, we just hang out with some pizza, when it's not so damn hot out.

HOW THE JELLYFISH WISHES

The farmer's boy was born in a season of drought
and dreamed nightly of the western coastline
where it was rumored
that all the stars were migrating
to crash into the sea.

No one knew why this was happening,
but they accepted it.

He awoke with his body in the soft L shape of California
and began to pack.

He was through spending his life between harvesting sweat
and day-gazing upon the scalp of the horizon
for something that felt like home.

He grew up working the soil
and understood that he was like a crop,
that he was just a patch of minerals that rose from the earth
and demanded water and light.
Crops are based in seasons and transformation.

A life,
no different.

Corn was a maze his family had been lost in
for generations.
Some years it was beans.

"Everything changes in this farm but us.
Starlight has stopped visiting. I am going West to join it."

He would be the first to seek
the visions, rumored to be streaking light, spittering brightly
into the endless onyx arms
of the Pacific.

By dawn, he would not look back.

Orange buckets of light spilled a rusted dusk
across the maple and oaks of Tennessee.

The fields along his route sizzled
with the chamber music of cicadas and bullfrogs.
Possums went squinting at the cackled dawn.
Endless fences poked up like bad teeth in the sunlit mouth
of a fallen giant.

He raced away on a lazy train with eighty dollars crumpled
and a journal.

Lightning had slammed its brights on outside
as he skimmed earlier entries:
"None of the teachers could explain why
the stars were migrating west.
The word on the street was that some states had fallen
into a season of mental drought,
where people stopped moving their beds near windows.
They settled into dreaming of bills, tanning salon gift cards
and affordable karate practice.
They stopped wishing.
There was no work for stars here."

When he reached the sea he found headlines in the *LA Times*
stating a theory that the stars had come to light the sea. To reveal.

It was true. The stars bolted down the highways of night sky
and steam-burst
into the waves. Glowing their metal and rock into
cannonball breaches.

They looked like lighthouses being flung into the deep.

How do we know this came to pass? You could see it all.

Have you heard of fish that wish for wings near Avalon harbor?
You can watch them lift into aerials like fat finches.
Have you heard of diatoms that wish for their remains
not to be scattered
but to be used in dynamite and toothpaste? The gardens!
The jellyfish wish their hearts to become luminescent.

Some bland fish wish for only the skin of a rainbow.
Have you heard of the humpbacks who wish
for the ability to sing for 10 hours straight
to serenade their families swimming back home
to the sound of their voice?
Tiny creatures, tired of their fins, asking
to become horses of the sea and they got it.
They all got it because they asked.
Because they don't know what silly is.

And who among us has not wished for the sky to come
and show us something?

And how many are waiting and wishing into that sky for relief?

The farmers boy always wished he could sing.
He dove in.

You could see him underwater.
You could see everything around him.

THE VICTORY EXPLOSIONS

I try to remember my youth.
It evaporates into 76 memories.

One memory was that you believed
the earth was made perfect by God
and that humans fouled it up
and that sin was something we gave birth to,
as God shook his head at our idiocy.
"How could they choose terror and loss?"

I don't think God really ever wanted perfection
if he designed the things he made with an instinct to screw up.

Fighting it and failing is beautiful and hard.
Screwing up is part of the program. Call it sin. Call it human.
Maybe there are codes built inside of darkness needing light
and vice versa.

It did not shake your belief in the existence of a God,
but it shook your belief in the bland necessity for perfection.

It birthed the belief that the human who could figure out
the balance of a hunger for winning and a deep respect for losing
would win the life trophy.

You go back to the first year you learned to daydream in a clothing
rack.
The first year butterflies bloomed adrenalized
in your wet guts.
In the 5th grade, you tempted everything.
Bicycles spinning,
the smell of girls,
pencils at war,
dismantled radios.

Launching off the swing set into the air, your first sensation of flight.
An innocent season for getting your ass kicked by a boy
who thought it would be a nice sign of his love.

Adam White and I liked the same girl. He heard I'd kissed her
underwater at her Dutch pool party, French
style, which is weird for a 5th grader like me.
I had not even kissed Snoopy.
These were skill sets as a 5th grader my tongue was not prepared for.
I did not know who started the rumor,
but I was about to pay for it with the cash of my face.

The same field we chased girls together in,
the strong, freckled Adam challenged me to my first fistfight.
I felt like a coward in a costume of a coward.
I was skinnier than a dead model.

No matter how much I denied the rumor,
his freckles kept popping from his face like braille.
"Your ass is grass, Derrick Brown."

I know.

The crowd gathered.
I stared at them like a sparrow trapped in an airport terminal,
wanting sky but stuck against glass.

I stood like a cricket in a junkyard of fiddles
unable to stop my legs from shaking music from my knees.

He swore he loved her, and that I would pay.
His forehead blistering
wrinkling like a crumpled valentine.

Where in the hell were the teachers?
What I wanted was mercy,
but even I didn't know what that word meant.

His fist came out and crushed at my jaw.
My eyes went black and all that I saw
was a shower of lightning bugs.
Children flashing into sunshine.
My teeth penetrating my cheek.
Falling backwards,
blood fertilizing the softball field.

But instead of freezing, I stood up again.
He struck me down, once more.
Eyes, ricocheting against the back of my skull.
The earth, meeting my failure, legs buckling,
skin reeking with contact, and I stood up again.

And he socked me with all his might.
Matchsticks lighting in my cheeks.

And I stood up again.

And he hit me so hard my Mother's eyes bled.
And I fell again, and I stood up again, and again, and again, and
again,
until he grew tired of socking me and left. Everyone left.

Alone there, baptized in my own warm blood,
I now knew the cost of the satin sponge and slop of a girl's ridiculous
lips.
'Cause guess what?
We did kiss under water at that Dutch pool party
like aqua spies and it was worth it.

There's nothing for me to learn from winning.

 It is losing that has yielded the unforgettable lessons.

Losing is pregnant with chance.
Victory escorts loss to every dance.

Harmony,
harmony.

THE TIMING OF CAROL AND WALT

Some folks called him Dirty Walt because he never cussed.

His wife was just Carol.

I called them Grandma and Grandpa even though we weren't blood.

Walt was a co-worker with my Father
at the Long Beach Shipyards.

I mentioned that I overheard his nickname at Thanksgiving once
and took a good beating for that. I didn't know it was bad.

I often wished I could live with the couple to see how they became
one person.

I have heard of women who cohabitate
and magically link their biological clocks.
I have heard of lovers passing away at the same time.

I have heard of teammates knowing where the pass was going
to go before it was sent.

That strange power was evident in Carol and Walt.
They were connected like twins, exchanging ends of sentences.
They would take RV trips everywhere
and would sense when the other needed to stop to pee
or rummage through a thrift store.

They got sick around the same time a few years ago.
They stayed in the same hospital in Sun City.
I don't know what Walt's illness was. Cruel.
Grandma Carol was fighting the mechanism in her throat.
She spoke like a broken machine.
She was tired of this non-living.

At her funeral, I remember her hands and feeling the loads of makeup
upon them. They wheeled Grandpa Walt in.
I had never seen this icon wheeled anywhere.
They rolled him up to the casket as the nurse held his IV.

His body, crumbling.

For me, every inch of his body was a home movie
of a man cutting turkey,
a man laughing at a renegade fart,
a man swinging me in the avocado tree.

He sat hunched over, emaciated and unable to form sentences.

Someone who didn't know how to control their children
let their kid run up and say, "Hi, Hi!"
The kid was laughing and patting him on the back.

He didn't know he was doing anything wrong,
like a little boy.

The Mother and Father oblivious.
Walt could not respond.
He stared into the casket the way a fisherman stares deep into a pond.

I wanted to tell the kid, "Give him some dignity,"
but I don't know how to explain things to kids.

The nurse, trying to stop him from standing, was overpowered
by his determination.
Grandpa Walt stood up, trying to disconnect his nasal tubes,
pushing away the nurse.
He stood and leaned over into the gray casket and
said something everyone heard.
"I will see you soon, my love."

His wheelchair cranked as he stumbled back into it.
They knew when each other wanted to stop.

From where I was sitting, I could not see her,
but I could see the shape of the light around her.

IN DEFENSE OF SLEEP CONTROL
for JB

All hail the rise of the Chest Tenderizer,
Invisible Friend of the Swallows,
Night Primer, Reverence Combuster,
Horror Choke.

How lucky I am to live this day
far from the lazy noose of the Tennessee Moon,
far from the cold hiss and clacking masts of Nowhere Bay,
far from the Carolina buzz of bullets and foxhole pestilence,
close to the thin arms of you.

Your engine cooing, purr-purr of deep rest.
The coiled lover, defending herself in sleep.
You are this dream of transparent blouses.

We watch our lovers in this state, speaking words into their hair
to shape the mares. To load their days with impulses
and notions they will feel as their own.

I whisper:
You came as vibrant Aster,
drunk lamp lighter, igniting wild the fences.
Kiss cloaker, Sexually crippling, shin shattering beast of gladness.
A full flask for a death bed.
Unable to un-gorgeous or disrobe your symmetry.
May your morning lips volley their rain and saffron down upon my
tin thin skull.
May your legs out-soft the others.

How you rest like a love among brothers.

So lie long
as I breathe upon you these small songs.
I exhale across your neck so you may find your nightmare maze
breezed open
through the tall fields of the now bowing wheat.

I will cover you with the down and you will feel
the sun warm through the Godless tundra
of your second dream. When you wake,
you will give me five dollars for no reason.

I will kiss your shoulder
and the vultures in your slumber
are chased by millions of smaller birds
scrambled into a bazaar of flight.
So many birds, with yellow eyes,
above becomes a starlit night.

I whisper:
Dawn Primer, Daylily Combuster, Horror Choke.
Gloom Tenderizer, Invisible Friend of the Swallows.

Let me in. Let me in.

THE LAST POEM ABOUT ANNE SEXTON

There must have been a moment when she thought
about the photo of her daughter
on the hallway mantle.

The kid.

Listening to the car gargle in that swampy garage.
The door locked.

Garden hose crammed up the cunt of the exhaust pipe.
Sitting there in the drunken shade of irreversible.

All the film negatives in the house of family photos,
melting.

To know that she had to choose and to know what she chose
makes me wonder about people.

It makes me wonder most about her daughter, if she can get up off
her knees.
Not clench her teeth every time she holds a hose.
Watering the lilies.
Hoping next year's annuals will last longer than this.

This came to me in a sweat and kept me up
the way Jesus stayed up the night he saw how
he was going home.

LISTING MY CONFLICTS WHILE DRIVING TO VALHALLA

The only thing worth writing about is the human heart in conflict with itself.
—William Faulkner

It's OK to be nothing to everyone else
if you are everything to someone else,
especially when everyone you know keeps treating the little nothings
like it was everything.

I am from everywhere I've been
and everywhere else feels like nowhere
when you are where
I am not.

There are a million living poets better than I,
but I have a million poets living inside.
What to feed them!

If Jesus is God then he actually said this,
"I am the way, the truth and the life. No man comes to me except
through me.
          Dear me, take this cup from me."
I have been that vain.

I could use some religion that is in no way religious. You'll do.

The older and deafer I get, the more I
need the screaming.

I like the quiet but I wasn't born quiet, I was born screaming.

My Speech to The Graduating Class

For the advancing friends at the High School in Ashburn, VA.

I might have written it somewhere else, maybe in another poem, but
it might be a nice way to start off this
shindig.

You belong everywhere.

The age you are at right now is something you will want back in
about ten years. Try to be less reserved. Be bold now. Tell her you've
got a crush, or had a crush and if they make the right face then you
can still have that crush. It's OK. She won't stab your face. They
may not reciprocate. Lose sometimes. Learn to love to lose. It makes
winning juicier.

This is a neat era, the age of exploration. I was a desperate explorer. I
ain't talking about Robitussin overdoses and turning an apple into a
bong. I am talking exploring limits and setting your boundaries.

I am talking about toilet papering someone's house you love that
doesn't own a revolver. Ding dong ditching the mayor. Run through
the golf course at night hunting for your balls. The parents will for-
give you. The cops will forget you. You are young and that has value.
And the value is a bail amount randomly set by a bored judge.

Get a journal. You should document this moment because the up-
coming changes are shocking. Punks will become political activists
in suits, Hippies will become business people for environmental
agencies, Skaters will become graphic designers, Football stars will
become glow in the dark pastors, Band kids will become ninjas,
Cheerleaders will become sad moms. Maybe journal it all because
you will forget. The future will seem so different. Teens in the future
are going to listen to subterranean carnival music, or boxes rubbing
together and you'll say, "...aw back in my day, we sang like idiots,
with our mouths."

No matter how cool you were at your coolest peak of high school,
in 4 years you will look back at photos and say, "Lordy I was a big
dork." You're not a dork. But you'll think that. It's OK. This will
give you the rush of humility.

This is good. Be proud of how humble you can be.

Some of you are off to college. Screw you.

College is not a passport to success. A passport is not a passport to success. Delaying self-gratification is. Credit card problems, managing money and taxes, all that.

Learn how to not want it now. Studies show that the main thing that plagues our generation is that we don't know how to delay self-gratification. If you can learn to save money, organize a game plan, read, clean up our lives, floss once in awhile, pick up your crap, then you will rule your world.

You will forget your locker combos, the concept of popularity and the valedictorian's speech. You will remember the teachers who cared for you and you will remember being able to eat Taco Bell like an aardvark without barfing up any ants.

You want to be a doctor. You might end up working at Chili's. At least for a while. So what? Try the steak fajita pita. You're working and there is honor in labor.

There are jobs out there you don't have to hate. You will hate your first few jobs. Pretend it's a game. Pretend you love hardship. "You want me to stay an extra hour? How about two hours you whacko!" Make sure you collect your overtime. The Crazies have power. Write stuff down. Make lists. It feels good to cross things off your list.

Let's not be scared about the future. Let's be scared about our bodies getting even wonkier and weirder. The unexpected fart is the blue ribbon of old age. It's all fine.

The Military is not what they are telling you. It can change you for the better. It can change you for the worse. It will definitely let you shower with many naked people. At once. It will help you kill most fears. They may offer you job or location. The job you get in the military is more important than the location. You can deal with a doo-doo location.

The end of high school is not freedom. A soaring, screaming, bald eagle with a cape and a laser frisbee is.

It is as hard to forget the bad stuff as it is to remember the good stuff. You will forget a lot about this time. Remember the hallway make outs. Forget the wedgies. Most bullies end up on court TV anyway, losing. Most jerks start to feel bad around 26, so let them molt that jerk skin and feel mercy for the secrets they are burdened with.

Forget all that crap about the journey, not the destination. Learn how to meet good people, try and remember their names and treat them well. Die happy if you die surrounded. You will forget people's names. Only jerks don't understand this. A jerk says, "Um, yeah. We met. Already, so…"

Really cool people don't know they are cool. There was a whole lot of hunger to be myself when I got out of High School and I longed to be known as someone who broke conformity but I dressed like all my friends. Or friend.

Some people in college may get drunk and try to kick your face in. Know when to kick back and know when to tell your friends you punched someone's foot with your face.

Even drug dealers think users are annoying.

Don't think about sex more than you have to. Your parents think you don't ever touch anybody. Help them with that lie.

As far as writing a virginity pact: you don't need some pact to stay a virgin if that's your thing. Over 14,000 get busy after the first year of making a virginity pact. A pact or vow does nothing if you are lying to yourself. Also, SEX CAN SCREW YOU UP IF YOU HAVE TOO MUCH TOO EARLY WITH THE WRONG PEOPLE. Treat it like lobster. If you have lobster all the time, no one cares about the joys of lobster. Make sure your stomach is ready for lobster. You don't want to have your first lobster at a fast food place. I do wish there was fast food lobster though.

A grad speaker once said wear sunscreen. I would like to add to please don't use the sunscreen that stays white on your nose. It looks like you cried glue and are too sad to lift your arms.

Learn something every year or your mind will die at a television altar. If your friend gets cancer treatment, learn everything about it and shave your head. You may find a lesion.

Young love has about a 20% chance of success. Unless you're in the South where it is mandatory to get married at 19. Try to not get so broken up about it. You're learning. Young love is real. So is future love and future love kicks more ass. There is more than one. Heartbreak makes you funny. Learn what you need.

Kiss with all your might. Then mix it up. Everyone loves a weird kiss! Even your dog.

Tell strangers nice things about their eyes or clothes. You will change their day.

Some people are drawn to drama. You are not community theater. Fire the actors from your life. Just 'cause you know someone doesn't mean you owe them anything. Especially if they're a tool.

Ladies. Tell men exactly what you want. They are simple creatures. They do not read into things. Take him to dinner. Gentlemen. Tell her how you feel, a lot. Notice details about her and tell her you noticed it. Ask questions and just listen. Hug her a little longer than your friends. Plan things. Plan thoughtful things. You still might get it wrong. But you tried and that's everything.

Now the work force. If you don't know what you want to be, so what. You will fall into something. Just do something that gives you a tiny thrill or you're just a gassy little speed bump. You want to be an artist or photographer, or writer? Don't worry about being good, just begin. Fear of starting has ruined so many potential pieces of waiting, great art.

Realize that guilt has guided very smart people in the wrong direction. There is no room for guilt in your crowded factory of creation.

It's crazy that you're here. Imagine what it is like raising kids. Know that it's hard. Let your parents know you know this. They may cry. Being alive is expensive and they wanted you more than those fancy romantic private vacations. This should make you feel good, the knowledge that you ruined a lot of fun by coming to this planet.

But maybe you're better than fun?
Always have poor friends or acquaintances. If you don't have any, go to a poetry show. The purchasing of useless gadgetry feels ridiculous when people close to you are desperate.

Some people aren't very good at laughing. They will be mad at you. Wonder how they got that way and keep laughing. Maybe not in their face. No one loves a spittle spaz.

Ask old people how they're doing. The answer will be long. This will help you slow down.

Go to other countries. Not a typical backpacking tour. Planned tour means you will hang with Americans on bikes and flirt with drunk Germans and someone will steal your Levi's in the hostel and a guy from Poland will sock you in the face while bad techno plays everywhere and you will learn nothing except that the Poles have a great left hook and not everyone on the bus showers. Get into other cultures and talk politics, God and love. It is the best church.

Meeting other people is the only way to know if you believe what you believe 'cause it's been handed to you, or if it really rings true in your heart.

Getting lost should be seen as a sweet chance to be found.

Remember, you belong everywhere.

Born in Year of the Butterfly Knife

A Finger, Two Dots, Then Me

Lying together in the park on Seventh,
our backs smoosh grass and I say
I will love you till I become a child again,
when feeding me and bathing me
are no longer romantic,
but rather necessary.

I will love you till there is no till.
Till I die.
And when that electroencephalogram shuts down,
that's when the real lovin' kicks in.

Forgive me for sounding selfish
but I won't be able to wait under the earth for you

I will not be able to wait for you—

but I will meet up with you,
and here's where you will find me:
get a pen—

Hold your finger up
(two fingers if your hands are frail by now)
and count two stars directly to the left
of the North American moon.

You will find me there.
You will find me darting behind amazing quasars
beyond flirtatious winks
of bright and blasting boom stars!

Sometimes charging so far into space
the darkness goes — blue.

I will be there chasing sound waves,
riding them like two-dollar pony ride horses
that have finally broken free and wild.
I will be facing backwards, lying sideways,
no hands, sidesaddle, sometimes standing
sometimes screaming zip zang zowie!

My God, it's good to be back in space. Where is everybody?

You will recognize my voice.
You will see the flash of a fire trail
burning off the back of me
burning like a gasoline comet kerosene sapphire.
This is my voice.

Don't look for my body or a ghost.

I'll resemble more a pilot light than a man now.

I'm sure some will see
this cobalt star white light from earth
and cast me a wish like a wonder bomb.
And I'll think "Hmm. People still do that? Good."

I'm sure I'll take the light wonder bombs
to the point in the universe
where sound does end.

The back porch of God's summer home.

It's so quiet, you float.
It feels the way cotton candy tastes.

I say to him, "Why do I call you God?"
He says, "Because Grand Poobah sounds ridiculous."
(Who knew He was so witty?)
I ask him, "Lord, so many poets have tried to nail it—
Ginsberg, Corso—and missed.
What is holy? What is actually holy?"

At that moment,
the planets begin to spin and awaken
and large movie screens appear on Mars, Saturn and Venus,
each bearing images I have witnessed
and over each and every clip flashes the word

holy.

armadillos—holy
magic tricks—holy
cows' tongues—holy
snowballs upside the head—holy
clumsy first kisses—holy
sneaking into the movies—holy
your mother teaching you to slow dance—holy
the fear returning—holy
the fear overcome—holy
eating top ramen on upside-down frisbees
'cause it was either buy plates or more beer—holy
beach cruiser nights—holy
the $5.00 you made in Vegas
and the $450.00 you lost—holy
the last time you were nervous holding hands—holy
feeling God at a pool hall but not church—holy
sleeping during your uncle's memorized dinner prayer—holy
losing your watch in the waves and all that signifies—holy
the day you got to really speak to your father 'cause the television
broke—holy
the day your grandmother told you something meaningful
'cause she was dying—holy

the medicine
the hope
the blood
the fear
the trust
the crush
the work
the loss
the love
the test
the birth
the end
the finale
the design
in the stars
is the same
in our hearts

the design
in the stars
is the same
in our hearts

in the rebuilt machinery of our hearts.

So Love, you should know what to look for
and exactly where to go.

Take your time and don't worry about getting lost.
You'll find me
up there, a finger and two dots away.
If you're wondering if I'll still be able to hold you
I honestly don't know.

But I do know that I could still fall for
a swish of light that comes barreling
and cascading towards me.
It will resemble your sweet definite hands.

The universe will bend.

The planets will bow

and I will say,
"Oh, there you are.
Now we can go."

And the two pilot lights go zooooooooom
into the black construction paper night

as somewhere else
two other lovers lie down on their backs and say,
"What the heck was that?"

Waltzing The Hurricane

If women only knew how dyslexic they can turn men by only holding their gaze on them for a few extra seconds.

Waterslide architects have been spying
the smooth of your back,
mapping blueprints
from the finger trails
adoring up your spine,
stealing your sleek design.

In this light
I can see through your body.
'Portuguese Man-of-war' as Woman.
Enemies sliced by the electric wit in your lipstick.

You are a Sunday porch I could do nothing on
and feel like everything was happening.

Let me pull my hurricane move—
a move to turn your gilded fortress to shrapnel—
to wind scorch your overbooked rickshaws,
melting your slippers into glass formula.
Girling you out.
Bursting your leggings
into pink shredded wheat.
AAAAAAH!

Andromeda Carnivora
envy of novas
zing your flesh across twilight.

Stay asleep
so the aircrafts aren't drawn to land
on the Christmas lights
crackling safety signals
from your eyes.

I saw you
panting in the oven of your skin.
Aren't you tired of awakening next to lost armies?
Sick of people looking for jade in your nostrils?

Subterranean teeth-gnashing orchestra.
Zebra killer.
Flexed duchess.
Carved cha-cha-cha.
Zirconia sass rock.

I want the theater without the drama.
I want the opera without the soap.

Lay in the stillness of a fighting-saints fairy tale.

Your partner is here,
a frog in a coma of kisses.
You, dressed as wonder,
screwed me backwards
with your
dyslexic kiss.

Fairytale saints fighting a stillness.
Kisses of coma.
Here is partner your.
Wonder dressed you.
Backwards me screwed.
Kiss dyslexic.

Come Alive

Citizens of Narnia:
I must admit
I was a reluctant candidate for Mayor.
I have shaken the hands
and hooves of many
throughout this great land

And I must admit
for many, the beat inside has died.

A great sorrow overwhelms me
for even the drums inside my chest
are growing quieter each day.

When did we become a library of children,
shelved like great novels
no one had time to read?

As Mayor of Narnia
I declare that this day must be the day we come alive.
I will declare a day for dipping our hands in butter
so we can practice letting go of what we were
and watch our hands emerge as telephones
so we can know our true calling.

Brrrrrng. It's for you. It's the future!

As Mayor of Narnia,
I will declare a day of common sense
on behalf of North American waiters everywhere.
If you can't tip 20%
then you don't get to go out to eat
and you don't get to make babies
'cause you have no baby makin' common sense.

As Mayor of Narnia
I declare a day for talking to the trees.
What are they saying? They're saying "Climb me,
carve your future lover's initials into my spine,
sacrifice me for your books.

Every book, every page is my blood. I give this to you.
If it's a war for the lands of imagination, I am ready to die."

They're saying,
"Go ahead—get young as your brain thinks you are on this day.

Invite snow angels to a bonfire
and give them s'more-flavored popsicles.

Buy cereal with the worst nutritional value
but the biggest prize.
Go meet your prize.

Sing and misplace your keys.

We're gonna fly kites in reverse
with the sail planted firmly in the soil
and our bodies on a string
sculpting clouds into the faces of people we miss.

We're gonna make thank-you cards
and rest them on soldiers' graves.

We're gonna raise a hand
in the back of the world classroom
and the answer we come up with
is to pull the night down
stare stars in the face
and reclaim lost wishes.

We're gonna capture the details.
We're gonna turn off the machines.

We are no longer waiting.
We are not the dishes we pass.
We are the passion we dish.

If you've been away from Narnia for a while, welcome back.

The kingdom is outside.
The kingdom is inside.
Today is the day we must come alive."

Amazing Jim Number Nine and Seven

*This is the first poem I ever wrote that I really felt good about, around '95-
'96. I performed it in 1998 at the Paramount Theater in Austin. I have never
heard a thousand people stay perfectly still. I also felt like an ass for shaking so
hard from being nervous and from having a bad handlebar moustache.*

I'm 23. She's 25.

"When you lie on your back, your voice sounds different.
I feel like a cloud."

Oh. I've made a woman giddy. Talkative. *Abierto.*

She used to get her hairspray confused with her deodorant.
How supermarket-hygiene-aisle-Brazil-iant her locks would smell
and how salon-style-sticky her clean American armpits would feel.

I hear her words like a toddler
with floaties
bobbling in blue illuminated night pools.

      "Sticky
Uncomfortable but still
      I could never
Horse glue
      Clumsiest bike"

Something about how she could never do this trick
where you throw your kickstand down as you roll to a stop.
She said she fell like a heavy pancake,
like Jenga in slow-mo.

Lips movin' arms goin' throwin' her kickstand down.

—Now, a slow hollow sound.

I didn't bring all this home.
Those pop metaphors.
Those Aqua Net armpits.
Those kickstand fingers flicking my chest.

I lie inches from beautiful bedhead
moonshining hair
500,000 filaments burning.

I cannot cuddle with someone's history.
It takes the anonymity away.
Like hearing a magician's real name.
Like seeing a clown without make-up.
Like honest touch.

How can you hold that?
How could these skinny arms hold all that?
All her clumsy history is kicking my ass.
She pinches my elbow skin.
She says, "Amazing. I remember being nine years old and thinking,
wow, there's no nerves there. Amazing."

I say, "Amazing, I can't feel a thing."

What is the name of that perfect nerve
that tells your eyes to shut tight when pain approaches?

Jim.
Amazing Jim, the magician.

Eyes synchronize shut and now I am no longer here.
No longer bobbling and floating.
Steady.   Running.

Running alongside her.
Slowing her down by gripping the back of the banana seat.

Throw your kickstand down—now!

And I'm wrong
and we fall
we fall together
over the spokes
and I feel the spokes
I feel 'em. The dirt.

And for as long as they remain shut
I am seven and she is nine.

"I feel like a cloud," she says.
And I know this is true
for I know the terrible things that go on inside of clouds.

That night drags its nails down the wall
and it sounds like—

Thirteen Piece of Electrical Tape

1.
The average amount of spiders
someone always swallows in their lifetime
is ten.

I am part of a study
to determine the amount of kisses
dogs attempt to steal from us in our sleep
in a lifetime

but you can't know the results until I die.

2.
So as I'm pouring sugar all over this woman's body
She says Ooooo. Nummy nummy.
Pouring sugar all over my tummy. I want more!
Make me hot and weird, you son of a bitch!

And that's when I pull down the blowtorch mask and holler,
crème brûlée!

3.
Rebecca, there's something funny and heavy about a girl
with dyed black hair
and a scar on each wrist.

I always say, "Hey, you're supposed to put perfume there."

4.
Those little skirts that are really just shorts
with a flap in the front
just piss me off.

It's deceitful and you know it.

5.
The cops are everywhere
and some are wearing uniforms. I hear it's a hard job
to not unload your whole clip. I hear it's a hard job
to unload your clip into their legs so they can testify.

6.
There will come a night
when the whole world falls asleep
at the same exact moment
and no one will be guarding the banks
or malls
or jewelry shops
and that's a great time
to sneak into the movies
if you know how to run a projector.

7.
I lay the same piece of electric tape
over every lover's mouth.

It isn't so sticky anymore.

I wish it wasn't losing its ability to stay.

8.
A kid named Hector said to me,
"Hey, I got a penny in my shoe."
I asked him if that got a little irritating.
He said, "No. They're lucky pennies, silly."
That's all anyone can learn from dumbass Hector.

9.
So girl,
What do you like to do?
Do? Um, I dunno. Second base, maybe third.
I meant what do you like to do here in Long Beach?
Oh. You mean—Oh. Third base.

10.
Mass confusion
might have something to do with the Puns running Catholicism.

11.
A man buried his imagination yesterday.
Took the job. At this age, I totally understand.

12.
Actually, your speed will not be detected by aircraft radar.
I've never got a ticket.
I would prefer a zero tolerance policy where if you go 11 mph over,
decimated.

13.
My Russian jewel.
These hands turn to Sue Bee honey
and my nails flip to reveal pink crescent moons
when I think of our first night together.
Will it be like a tornado of sheets?
Or timed with the cadence of drooling candles
and the bass of pile drivers?
Wild enough to embarrass the furniture.

Woman girl, I want to hold you
the way grasshoppers
hold onto their bows.
The way Russia holds all the sad diamonds.
The way sand creatures hold down sailors' bodies.
The way children hold onto pennies and secrets.
The pool is filling with American horror.
I cannot let go of my weight.
So why not get married?
Is it fair to say I might not want to make love on honeymoon night?
Because I might be sore from doing it with you all day
in the train,
under the reception table,
dangling from the helicopter skid like a stuntman from the Kama
Sutra,
and in every public restroom we stop at from here
throughout all of North America
'cause I'm kinda romantic.

So instead,
that night,
we'll just have to sit there.
Speak about all the pieces of electrical tape we ever slept with
and wish we had never touched
anyone else.

PUSSYCAT INTERSTELLAR NAKED HOTROD MOFO LADYBUG LUSTBLASTER!

This poem was inspired by a Sparklehorse song and a Pavement song.
Hence the sparrow reference for Sparklehorse and the 66 shades of black for
Pavement. "Because there's 40 different shades of black, so many fortresses and
ways to attack..." Mine is 66 'cause of a road trip listening to that album.
Never ask your lover to write you a poem. It's like asking sperm to hurry up
and be a baby.

pussycat interstellar naked etc. etc.

how silly i get.
how lost and silly i get
unraveling my fingers
to where your arms connect.

i come to your body as a tourist.
endless rolls of black and wine film in my fingertips
documenting the places that change your breathing
when touched with the patience of glaciers retreating drip by drip.
it reverses your breath back into the places
that trigger subtle curls in your purple painted toes.

the breaths are not worth hundreds of sparrows
they are worth all the gray air sparrows die and wander in.

there are things about you i collect and sell to no one.
i journal them in a book you gave me with the inscription,

'don't leave your ribcage in the icicle air. something will break.'

i wrote about the courage my hand would need
aiming down the worn comfort of your hair,
hang-gliding across the summer slits of your winter dress,
searching the perfection in your rock-and-roll breasts,
stealing the heat off the drug of your stomach.

let me die a White Fang death
trembling on the snow and linen of your shoulder blades.

i want to buy you a black car
in 66 shades of black
to match the wandering walls of your heart
filled with the mysteries of space and murder in space.

let me spend my days on the shores of abalone cove island
collecting bottles that wash ashore
and burning the messages inside
to fill them with new messages like
"send more coconuts" or
"send more coconuts and wild boar repellant. i'm re-reading lord of
the flies." or

"wow, I'm actually on an island. please send my five favorite albums.
i've already built a victrola out of sand and eel poops.
it's the macgyver in me. this volleyball won't shut up."

i will float the armada of messages towards the atlantic
and wonder if a pale girl in new york spends time at the shore.

i will wonder if she can see the stars i carved our initials into
when I got sick and weightless.

lie in bryant park and look hard into the air.
your last initial isn't up there
for it is worthless to me
since i had dreamed of changing it.

this is the trunk sap tapped.
this is love of mercenaries.
i'd kill an army of sleeping cubans for the rum desires
in the clutch of your tongue.

touché to your lips!
touché to your way!
touché to your ass!

you are an electric chair disguised as a la–z–boy recliner
and i find comfort in you.

my clear bones take shape in the mouth of glassblower with asthma
for there is no perfection in me but maybe clarity.

crush me with the satisfaction of your black misted, unclocked
breath.
i always come back to the secrets and wonder of your breath.
it is something for sparrows to wander in.

it's not that i wait for you.
it's that
my arms are doors i cannot close.

VENTOM

When a writer is wronged
in comes sweet, sweet shiv-in-the-spine revenge
in a public fashion.

You said, "Run like the wheelchair is calling.
Kiss hangmen 'cause nooses can't hold you.
Love like a leprous woman."

All of it—piss in the mouth of a Bedouin begging for water.

And let's talk about our so-called sex,
the sex—Ha!
The sex—was—was—beautiful and meaningful—but the lies!

Your vagina is a white lie.
Your vagina is Virginia spelled wrong and packed
with just as much boredom.
Your vagina is a body bag for fraternity dropouts and
once-hopeful fetuses.
Tear me from your Lizzie Borden modeling agency.
Tear me from that pink community axe wound forever.

How could you not tell me that they used to bottle your mother's
saliva
and use it to taint the punch at Jonestown?
Horns poking through your hairdo—Beelze-bob.

Your heart—colder than a necrophiliac's first entry.

Your pop astrology has already made your decisions for you.
Your sun is in drama.
Your moon is in bullshit and I can feel all the flags
planting into your dust.

I could use a bear rug
with your head in its mouth
to remind me that someone else
is tasting you right now, holding his breath.

This is my confession.
This is how I repent.
This is how I pretend to be OK
in a public fashion. Grief's bitch.

The polar bear rug misses his eyes
but most of all—misses the warmth and his insides.

How long must I wait covered in lemons,
crippled in this chalk outline,
unable to confess my part,
unable to trust my lonely music?

I am worn and unnoticed like the steps to a children's mortuary.

When the poetry vending machine breaks
all that comes is—I am so worn out.
I can't imagine learning someone all over again.
Despising her photos that crossfade into mirrors.

When you said you loved me so hard,
you'd kill for me,
I didn't know
it would hit
so close
to home.

The petrified forest is resolute and can not waver. I still love you.
So stick that up your ass.
The beautiful shit-purse you pulled forever out of;
your passionately unfaltering, wholly honest, naturally bleached ass.

THE LABRADOR IS POSED
IN THE FREEZER

Linda cannot look the panting German Shepherd in the face. It is
shaking like a young actor. Dogs shake at the veterinarian not be-
cause they are scared to die, but because they are scared to leave their
masters. *"I couldn't bear it if something happened to them if I was gone."*
Even if it's just a check-up, dogs smell death as well as they smell fear
and for Zinger, the pink smell has become strong.

Small room with doctor. Technician with black name-tag, Linda,
enters with customer. Customer folds her lips back into her mouth
and clutches her car keys, sets her purse upon the hairy, scratched tile.
Linda holds the animal in the aggressive posture, pinned like a Greco
champion. Shove forearm along back. Headlock. Hold down back
legs with left hand. Do not look the dog in the face. Customer is
crying like she is drowning. Shaking her head at this scene she never
imagined. Dog is pinned on counter atop green beach towel 'cause of
shit and piss.

"Would you like to say something, Ma'am?"

"Oh God. Jesus. Jesus Christ. Baby, I'm sorry. I'm sorry. I
couldn't—Aw jeez. I just couldn't afford the surgery. I'm sorry I'm
poor, baby. Maybe—a—took a double shift or more hours so—so—I
could—Jesus Christ."

"Ma'am?"

Breathing, breathing, house-key-hitting-car-key sounds. The dog
is trying to lunge but is too old to overpower Linda. The customer
stands up, hand on hip, and taps her foot nervously, takes a deep
breath to ready herself for a blow to the ribs, touches the dog on the
forehead and says in a soft, collected tone, "O.K."

Linda the technician can't help but look towards the back of the head
of the Shepherd. Its face tilts toward the owner. There is a whimper
and its sharp ears perk up. Not to say help me. Not to say I'm scared.
It says:

"Why? Why?"

Linda the tech sees the Shepherd's eyes. Linda cries, feeling the universal why and buries her face in the fabric softener smell of her lab coat.

The customer repeats "O.K. Good boy. Good Zing." and the Shepherd stops fidgeting. Still panting with its tongue out. The pink death is inserted into the artery near the leg. It's so efficient, seconds. The Shepherd is gone. There is piss. Dr. Matzko brings in a new towel. Ten minutes alone are granted and the woman, the customer, falls over the shell of her animal. *Don't go.*

In the hallway outside the small room, Dr. Matzko turns to Linda. "You cry every time, now."

"I can't help but look, doctor. I'm sorry. The eyes are getting me lately."

"The eyes of Zinger or the eyes of Mrs. Walker?"

"I go in there feeling strong as an ox. Then something happens where I just feel so much for certain animals, I imagine hanging onto that moment. Once they're gone, I can treat their carcasses like sleeping bags and it doesn't faze me. That table, the needle and everything lately—I think I can handle it and then something hits that trigger."

"I was like you in school, Linda. That's why I hired you. You've got a great heart for animals. Scott may be more composed, but I like your heart. The only thing I wonder about is that you seemed to have a better grip on yourself a few months ago."

"It's just a freak thing. I know it's unprofessional and I promise I'll get control of my emotions next time. Once again, I apologize." There is still sobbing coming from Mrs. Walker in the small room. With permission from Dr. Matzko, Linda goes home early, eats chunky ice cream, naps in a weird fetal position on her couch and returns several hours later for the night shift with fellow intern Scott Hornsby. When the long hours drag into the a.m., Linda pulls down her electronic keyboard from the bird food cabinet. She hits the demo button and moves her fingers across the keys. There is a harpsichord sound she likes.

They discuss what happened earlier that day, surrounded by medicine posters featuring Golden Retrievers. She finishes the story about the Walker lady. There is a long pause. They talk about Japanese ice cream. They talk about the problems of shooting the breeze and not learning anything. Scott reaches in the fridge. "This Dr. Pepper has your name on it but I think it belongs to Dr. Pepper." He chugs Linda's soda. "Heard you crazy cried today."

"I'd love to teach you something, Scott. I want you to remember something stark about life that will change you and make you less of an asshole." She only used the word asshole for people she was attracted to.

"Well, we got five-and-a-half more hours. I'm sure you'll think of something. Man. Still thirsty." He pulls two Pacifico beers out of the fridge from the dozen hiding behind the plasma.

"Let's see. I got a whole bunch of strange stuff. I could tell you about how to roll a cigarette with one hand, why people in Prague don't smile much, the importance of not listening to sad music on the way to the airport, how to punch someone in the throat with a lollipop stick. I could tell you now but you'd lose it. You should only tell people useful things right before you split. People only remember the beginning and the end." She flips the tone to electric piano on the control panel of her keyboard.

There was a long pause, which was acceptable 'cause there was music to fill the empty. She is mumbling lyrics. Scott watches her lips open and stick, a soft place.

Scott moves to kiss her while Linda stays as still as wax. Linda has locked her gaze at a spot on the floor. Scott touches her brown, un-styled hair. She freezes.

"Hey. Heeey. What's the matter?"

Linda speaks low towards the spot on the ground.

"I can't kiss you when I'm thinking. Do you think animals have souls? I'm not gonna get too crazy about it. I can't prove that anything has a soul. It's just what I have chosen to believe after looking these living things in the eye day after day; you know, healing them, helping them die.

Some so scared to go. Some dumb about it. Some at peace."

"Is there something you want to tell me?"

Linda starts breathing like the customer. Scott puts his hand to her back, trying to calm and holds her close.

"It's O.K., babe. It's O.K. Through your nose. Out your mouth. You're good."

He pulls back and looks her in the eye and sees a woman daydreaming of a place he can never visit. The feeling had choked the language from her.

She finally mumbles, "I wonder if when you name something, then it becomes real, or memorable. I wonder what a name does to a living thing."

Scott leans a mop across the white. "You sure do think of a lot of stuff when you ain't got shit to do. I brought you the good mop. Are you all right?"

"I just feel like talking. Like trying to figure this thing out."

"What thing? You look sick. Are you sick? I can get just about any pharmaceutical from Tijuana."

"No. I don't need you to solve. I just need you to listen." If Scott's brain had foley there would be a ding sound.

"Are you depressed? Are you quitting? Are you pregnant?"

Linda bit her teeth. She did not cry. "No. That's not it. I mean, I was. But."

The air became twelve thousand pounds. Scott was not bright, but he was a logical man. He slowed his tongue and waited to speak until his chest stopped feeling funny. He wanted to say why didn't you tell me? Did you lose it? Did you get rid of it? He wanted to say how dare you do this without me, but he knew he didn't know her well enough and probably would not love her. He turned to facts when he was lost.

"I read that animals abort spontaneously in stressful circumstances, without the grief that they show when a grown child dies."

Linda swabs at the tile. "You don't have to say anything if you don't know what to say. I'm fine."

"Was it scary?"

"No. Yes. I remember writing on my hand, 'I can hardly help dogs die, how can I help a human live?'"

Scott stood his mop at attention in the bucket and took a deep breath.

"God, I feel dumb right now. I feel like—like I want to take that from you. I know I can't. I know I can't do that. I just feel like sorry is such a dumb thing to say. I'll just stop talking. Should I hold you for a second?"

"I don't need that."

"Okay."

He opens his arms and covers her. She caves in and swallows him in her arms.

They held each other that evening, standing among the hairballs and dirty mop water of the animal shelter's lobby floor. A scene you will not imagine when you go to bring in your poodle for a vaccination. A scene that plays out differently in different places on different days throughout the world. People with different names wondering about the same things, while creatures with no names run around the wilderness, the air and the sea, loathing capture, needing no legacy, name or tombstone.

Here two forgettable, broken creatures stood, holding each other until the dogs, cats, birds and snakes lay down in their cages, held still for a moment, tired, their names locked around their necks, watching a moment unfold, unable to comprehend it but possibly remembering all of it.

Pleased to Meet You Yellow,
My Name is Blue

After reading in Laguna Beach, a woman came up to me and said "I liked your poem, but I used to live on a farm in Wisconsin and to tell you the truth, blueberries don't float." I said, "Well, to tell you the truth, I don't hover a few feet above the Pacific when I am sad. It's called suspension of disbelief. Get off me." This is one of the few poems I have memorized and I recited it to couples when I used to be a gondolier.
PS. Some less dense blueberries do float. Huzzah!

You came swiftly across the sea.
I hovered there,
thirty miles outside of Galapagos,
placed myself in the screams of rival winds.

I hovered there for years, alone,
feeding on everything blue:
shark fins, sea spray,
desire, memory and floating blueberries.

But you came swiftly across the sea,
took away my death (though I guarded it),
held my defeat by the neck and outsmarted it.
The ice in my breath floated before you
a crystal field of all my fears.
I was just getting used to the blueberries.

But you spun that warm ginger light.
Sent it spilling from the gold blaze of gasoline eyes.
Melted my breath.
Melted the soloist.
Melted the pumping thing inside.

You said, "Hello Blue, my name is Yellow."
and I said, "Wah. Wow."

I was stricken. I was struck.
I was a bad joke about a duck who was down on his luck
that no one ever laughs at—

but Yellow, she laughs—she's a laugher
and she's not even drunk!
I say, "Yeah Yeah!
I want to be something ridiculous and wonderful and Yellow."
She says, "Try margarine."

"No, I mean I want your firecracker smile, Yellow.
I want your jacaranda kiss, Yellow.
I want your timelessness
inside my eyeballs, Yellow."

The way snow falls to earth,
Yellow whispers to Blue—
"Would you be Green with me forever?"

"I do. I do. I do..."

Seven Years to Digest Gum

*This poem was born when I caught two shoplifting girls when I worked at a
magic shop at Knott's Berry Farm. The looks on their faces made me ache as
they aimlessly looked for receipts that didn't exist. It stays with me. This was
written while listening to my favorite band, the Afghan Whigs. Special thanks
to Greg Dulli for giving a rip about good lyrics.*

I have your gold, honey humper.
And guess what?

I swallowed it
'cause I read a book about internalizing self worth.
It said to keep something terrible inside me.
I swallowed your cool liquid gold.

It's dripping off my chin.
You want it?
Come and get it.

You want the dogs?
I'll cut 'em loose.
I've got a soundtrack of dogs crawling on their bellies.

The book said to build molds of beautiful marble hands
so you can practice letting the heavy go.
It said to drop them off buildings
and record the sound they make falling through the air.
Sound is something we can hold onto.
All my dead friends and lovers
are preaching through the wind in my ears.

Woman D6 chews gum in bed—
swallows it and talks of bad luck.
She says I lie in bed like a fallen statue.
Older women have taught me to hold still.

The rain tins down.
The grass will get so tall.
The dogs need a place to hide—
pretty dogs.

Her hovering screen-door-colored skin drapes me,
shadows melt down the wall,
we kiss in Spanish,
nothing is understood.

She has ascended,
trapped with the spine of her spirit
pressed to the roof.

An angel in amber
pulled by the warm steady light
the color of flat ginger soda. It will get you too.

The wind you will be someday. I hear it.
Pulled deep within my brain
you find my soundtracks.

I have a soundtrack of shoplifters
looking for their receipts.

I have a soundtrack of young women's throats
clearing in dressing rooms.

I have a soundtrack of bored jurors
thinking about sex,
crossing and uncrossing pantyhose across pantyhose.

I have a soundtrack of innocent men
hanging by their necks,
kicking their legs denim across denim.

I have a soundtrack of predators
caressing the hands of their prey.

I got a soundtrack of dogs
crawling on their bellies
low in the grass
moving towards the bird.

A soundtrack of doors only closing.

Spines banging against the ceiling.

A soundtrack with songs learned at birth.
A soundtrack of guardian angels swallowing sleeping pills.
A soundtrack of drool-slithering, creeping hounds, waiting for our meat.
A very catchy song
in a very catchy loop.

All my wind, trying to get out.

A soundtrack
rotating
in every miserable, merciless beast.

Medusa Oblongata

I wished to have had my love for you die first
like widows wished they would've perished first.

Every kiss was a chance to spit in your mouth.

Now you let your skirt fall like an empire to the beautiful armies
surrounding you.

Lead The Night's Commander, lead his tongue into the Nile.

Taste the meat around his teeth.

Promote his hands from your jowls to your breasts.

As he tries to beat the snakes out of your head and fails.

Drown him in this month's blood.

No matter how hard you drill,

Brother, you will not find oil.

Feel her sex go tepid once you show weakness.

Non-seduced spasmo-cadavers.

Pretend I no longer dwell in you.

I told you I'd return.

I am in his medicated thrust.

I am in his wallet as it buys your legs into the air.

I am his hiss crawling across your tonsils.

Call it what it is. Transactor.

When I said you were remarkable

I said real marketable.

Some churches are abandoned

but can't be torn down.

You are smoke. Smoke that can never return to the fire,
the fire you lift from until… nothing.

Why Amelia Earhart Wanted to Vanish

This is one of my favorite poems because Amelia is one of my favorite people ever to have graced the sky. I heard she had her first flight as a youth in Long Beach. She was kind of manly and severely beautiful and I would stare at her on the ceiling of the boat I lived on before falling asleep. I loved finding her in my sleep.

Amelia asks for forgiveness,
looks down at the table like we are playing chess.

The larger pout of her bottom lip is imported from
Uruguay: Ooo—doo—guy.
Her Rs and the As become dizzy ghosts when she says it.

Distance.

The bottom lip
simple as a sentence.
But the upper lip,
a complex creature.

Amelia's youth suitcased in the upper lip, ready for wrinkles.
Lipstuck lipstick lipstock residue in flushed hue
like she'd been kissing madly,
like she walked off the set of an MGM ending
cast to kiss sailors ready to die.

Some are ready to die.

Her hair looks as if she'd been running with a man in black and white
through the sets of dangerous cities.

Her few hard lines are just symptoms of sleeping on her face.
Amelia ruins pillowcases with her lipstick.

Zip focus into the darkness where her lips should meet.
God, those corners.

The black pockets—empty and full like poverty.

These are not simple.
Endless. Hungry. Surrounded.
Dragging air like jets of the atmosphere.
Drawing it in in slow motion,
drawing it in freehand
into those corner lip pockets.
The separations open and close
move elastic in melody with her chest.
1,2,3,4, 1,2,3,4 1—

Air marches in
and then nothing more marches out.

I could low-crawl inside those corner pockets,
grab her gums
to see if they're bleeding
to see if she wondered if she said the right thing,
to see if there was some sign of wonder or weakness or nervous,
the way dogs watch you after they've been hit by cars.

A sign that speaks of all normal persons having fear,
a bite in the cheek, a grind in the crowns
something that will give her away.
"C'mon, Amelia. Come on. This is not chess, Amelia."

She says "Shh. Save your yelling for sex and riots."

Peeking at the daylight from the corners of her mouth.
The dryness chaps.
I look for bats
or sailors' initials
but nothing.

For now it is dead in here.

I wait under the quilt of her tongue.
Unthawed.
Searching for blood.
Carving letters on her canines.
"Amelia. If you leave, don't you ever come back."

Alone in the cockpit, her propellers begin to spin.

12:55

This poem was inspired by the make-up I saw on a hand at a wake. I don't think many ever got the idea that in this poem, the clock hands at the 12:55 position look like they are hands raised toward the heavens.

You never thought a human hand could look like this.
Desert cracks.
Folds canyoned together by age.

Your fingertips slide across this fortune teller's nightmare.
You notice the bruised knuckles from the years he drove his fists into the walls
looking for answers.

The hands of a captain who lost the entire sea.

Now the smell enters you:

The air conditioning ducts pumping medicine,
the people of white aprons, their shoulders raised from the cold
and the motionless silver goodnight machines.

The cold, the white aprons, the blood and tools,
reminders of science class and butcher shops.

It hits you that this building
this room
was someone's last
toilet handle
last pillow
their last press on the power button
of a faded black remote control.

You feel sorry for the nurse that lost the draw and had to make the call.

"You must come, now. The doctor says 1–2 days tops."

You lean down.
His eyes haunt and float between two worlds.
He is your father, and you can't stop seeing him carry you on his back
through the blink of youth.

"I'd take ya for a piggyback ride kiddo, but I think it would kill me."
You laugh. He coughs. You wait.

His eyebrows lift.
They are your eyebrows.
Head tilts to see your face,
"Ya know, if there's one thing I wish I would've done in my life,
I wish I would've spent more time at the office, for you."

"Really, Dad?"
"Of course not, you moron. Don't be so moronic.
Drink your coffee, son. Don't waste it."

"You got me, Pop."

"Well, it's about time."

The clock hands at 12:55 a.m. look like they're surrendering
and you think to yourself
"This is bad coffee. My God, probably the worst.
How can they give him this shit?
Don't they know who he is?"

You drink it 'cause you get to drink together
and you hold his hand
wondering if anyone would notice
if you took him from this place
on your back.
You stretch.

A Few Things You Probably Already Knew About Emus

On the flight into Houston,
children sitting behind me realize that many words rhyme with turkey.
"Look, it's a flying turkey
No, it's a flying Turkey Murky Jerky!
No, it's a flying Murky Jerky Perky Lurky
Hurky Gurky Durky Quirky Furky Turkey."
I feel the Bloody Mary sizzling inside me.

Kids—What you're seeing is just an airplane.
What you're doing is pissing me off.
Have Daddy share some of the Ritalin he's been bogarting
before I go Monte Cristo and fry both of your hineys.
If you want to read or sleep, that's cool.
If you continue to irritate and rhyme all flight, I will eat you.
I will rock you, Amadeus!
I feel ill and if you don't calm down
I'll swallow both of you whole. Shhhh.

"Like Jonah."
What?
"Like Jonah in the whale?"
Sure.
"Like Jonah Mona Bona—"

Some children are of the corn.
They gave me something to concentrate on so I wouldn't vomit.
If only they knew I was concentrating on severing their tiny hearts.
Bye kids, take it easy.
"We're kids, we always take it easy!"

My father and stepmother Judy picked me up.
Tractor and trucking hats,
mesh and already sweaty.
A gift for the city boy.
I go to hug him.
I can tell it is a foreign move.
I squeeze even harder.
It's been two years since I've even touched him.

It's been 29 years since we've spoken.
Really spoken.

I heard the doctor spanked me good when I was born.
My dad got angry and shoved the shit outta him
and Pop held me in midair, without smiling,
without speaking.
I think this was the last time he held me.

His "Hello, I missed you," comes out as a hearty "Hey son. Let's eat!"

Texas is one big buffet. A world of Golden Corrals.
I watch the old me sneak Budweiser cans into the dining area.
They slip their cans from the secret pocket of their Sears overalls
And slowly open the tabs as if they were defusing bombs.

I go back for seconds.
Fried catfish.
Fried okra.
Fried rice and for an ethnic flair,
French fries!
Even the milk was fried.

Father lights a cigarette in my face. My chicken tastes like menthols.
We leave.

At my Father's trailer, there is a hired hand named Bob.
Bob went to Nam.
Bob says, "Navy nurse broke off a needle in my hip, for spite.
I did not like it."
You didn't?

"No, I didn't, but I threw my full bedpan at her, for spite."

Bob is addicted to alcohol.
Bob likes to draw.
Bob has Agent Orange.
Bob knows he's not very good at drawing.
Bob still draws.

A few things you didn't know about emus:

1. Best to kill and eat at 14 months.

2. Hard to take their eggs at night. My stepmother Judy has 20
stitches to prove it.

3. Natives of Australia. Dad says, "Aboriginals used them
for centuries."
I ask him if the ab-originals were the first people to do sit-ups.
He smiles.

4. 50,000 currently in the U.S. Dad says pretty soon they'll take
over, like the Mexicans. It's not meant in a racist way.

5. Their oils can make you better looking.

6. Tastes like unique beef.

Mowing lawns in Texas is much different than mowing lawns
on the sun, but only because
there is much more beer involved.
Bob actually fell off of his mower and accidentally
mowed a chicken.
My father was upset, not because something living had died,
he was upset because something he had paid for was gone.
Am I still talking about chicken?
Texas makes you know God resides among air conditioning.
My father won't buy air conditioning, but has a three-thousand dollar
satellite dish.
Judy asked me if I'd like to go to the supermarket.
I went for the AC.
The air in the store smelled like Antarctic blowjobs
and produce. Ahhhhh.

In the checkout line an elderly woman stands behind me
with a jug of punch.
I asked her where the wild party was.
She told me that her partying is like a dog chasin' a car, getting hit,
and still not knowin' how to drive.
I told her that if she wasn't a poet, she should be,
because I had no idea what the hell she was talking about.

When we come in from the market
I handed him his beers.
He handed me old Black Cat firecrackers.
We went outside.
I waited for the burden of conversation to come.
We pretty much just drank.
I almost blew off my thumb.
I kept the fireworks exploding in case he could hear what I was
thinking.
I wish I could forgive you—POW!
I wish there was no regret—POW!
I wish I could forgive you—POW!
You messed up—POW!

He breaks the rhythm:

"At one time, I had seven whores livin' in my trailer park.
One woulda been good for you. Little chubby, but she got a good
future as a dental assistant, even got her a new little Hyundai,
was doin' great, till she got on the hashish."

This was the deepest of our conversations and I still had not said much.

If you lose a remote control in Texas the channel will never change!
It is much too hot to be movin' around like a maniac, changin'
channels and all.
Madness.

"This is C-Span."
Silence.
"Do you like C-Span?"
Not in particular.
"Well, why are you watching it?"
Lost the remote.
"Well, I can get up and change it."
Now don't go acting like a maniac. I'm relaxing.

Later, he shows me how to use a power saw and tells me
when he was 23, he had to jump from a burning building
in San Francisco.
When he got to the fire escape, the people were yelling jump—
and there was nothing to jump into.

This happened when I hugged him.
Jump Jump Jump!
He still doesn't trust people.

"We honeymooned in Las Vegas, your real mother and me.
Told her to get away from the blackjack table cause she was bringin'
me bad luck."

He looks at me like I'm supposed to laugh
but it's much too funny to laugh.

Pow.

My father's words drop like white noise.

I let the dusk colors fall into me:
The seeping blue-eyed hunger of a faithful starving dog.
Fat garlic mosquitoes.
The boredom clouds of the hottest gray.
Sapphire sky shifts and the tall green blades sway, deep.

At the Fourth of July picnic
Uncle Cecil broke out his .22
and started a genocide for snapping turtles
pulled from the pond.

My cousin Tom threw me in the pond and my watch stopped.
I believe my watch stopped when I crossed into this state.

Every Church is a time Machine.
I visited a Church of Christ a few days earlier.
They don't believe in music
because the Bible doesn't say to have music.
My cousin Tom said, "The Bible doesn't say to wipe your crack,
but you still do!"
He gets a little preachy sometimes.

And there is the often quiet Uncle Cecil by the grill.
Tom tells me that Uncle Cecil doesn't come outside much
anymore.

Three years ago he watched his friend die in his arms
from a bee sting.
A damn bee sting.
The doctors told Cecil all he could've done to save him was to
break a pen in half and insert it into the front of his neck.
At the right spot he could've breathed again.
It sounds too dangerous to try and he just didn't know.
Cecil sure as hell knows how to do that now.
That kinda stuff happens in Texas.

It's hard to fall asleep in Texas.
The air is feisty,
thickens your blood.
I drink beers to fall asleep.
Dad says, "Goodnight, son. If we all die tomorrow,
at least you know I'm happy."
This scares me in a Jim Jones kinda way.

I turn the TV on through the night.
I leave it on a squiggly channel
for artistic reasons.

My stepmother wakes me by telling me,
"It's hotter than horny hogs in Hell's jalapeno hot tub."
She's right.

Judy pours herself some orange drink—
Cancer makes Coca-Cola taste crummy now.
She sure drinks a lot of it.

She says, "Do you wanna go to the mall? They got everything.
Let's roll!"
I ask the lady in the 99¢ store how much the rings cost.
She says 99¢.
I asked for any kind of interesting ring for my stepmother.
She slid me a pewter one of two people humping.
I said, "Interesting."

We roll down the windows on the way home.
The wind rips the scarf from Judy's head.
She grabs up and screams
and we swerve, almost into a ditch.

Look out! —"My scarf! I need…
Take the wheel—God—jeeeeez!"
We breathe.

She said she didn't want me to see her like that.
I tell her that many women movie stars in L.A.
shave their heads on purpose and I think it's pretty cool.
She says "really," like she was four and I had told her about Santa.

I felt sorry for my stepmother Judy,
not because of the cancer, but because of what her ring meant.
I wanted to replace it with my silly one.
She drives home kinda dangerous, as well she should.

It's hard to sleep again tonight.
Exotic dancers on TV are never down and never call.
As the beer makes me sleepy
I step outside
and stare at my watch
I piss into the 2:00 a.m.
and the forgiveness still waits inside my watch.

The trees outside here look dangerous.
Too dangerous.

I wish I could forgive you.
I wish there was no regret.
I wish I could forgive you.
I already said that.

MY TOMB

Love is the only war worth dying for.

Cursing Jeff Buckley

Most celebrity deaths feel like a publicity stunt and never touch me; Jeff had so many lines about shoes filling up with water and nightmares by the sea. What does it mean if your art tries to tell you how you will die? I read this poem in Munich and the bartender took me to the place down in the basement where Jeff had signed the wall a year or two earlier. He let me sign right next to it and it was an honor as much as it was strange. I fell for someone that night.

> *"I couldn't wait for the nightmare*
> *to suck me in and pull me under, pull me under."*
> — Jeff Buckley,
> three years before his drowning

You sultry poison.
You angel dust donor.
You American gunmetal tongue
stealing the power from women.

You said the nightmare sucked you in
and pulled you under.
The muck of the river filling your wide, shark-toothed mouth.
You cried out into the hard Southern night
and the moon is still helpless.

You held your breath
and went down.
Young body convulsing in the brackish water
shaking for life,
moaning for the surface June bugs.

Bubbles roared from your throat
filled with swirling notes of terror—
the last melody—the most beautiful.
You said the nightmare sucked you in
and pulled you under.

You died brilliant,
but how did you know?

A Short Song

Lo-fi ultra sound photo sat forever on your lap
like a war letter to a mother.

An infinite grief
wrapping your shoulders in a black mink
and dark ink.

The nauseous feeling left covert,
snuck from the theater of your gut, whisperless
and your new feeling of healthiness meant terrible news.

Like a lover with fists you will miss,
if you could still be sick for two more months
you would.

What do I say?

The vacancy signs of motels made you weep.
Secondary drumbeat please come in,
heaviness in your hollow,
a sleep that is breathless and safe.

No heartbreak, no failure, no words,
just fuzzy pictures and
the option of funeral
or leaving it at the hospital.

A doctor voicing it with the importance of fries or soup.

Maybe the child was too amazing for earth.
Maybe God is greedy.
Maybe the angel of death is as fast as a bored policeman
and just as dangerous.
Now you are tested and created to carry on, to begin again.

You were created for creation.
You are not a morgue.
You are a factory of mud fights and beauty
and if the assembly line goes on strike and crashes the machine of
your body

just negotiate with patience
and things may start running again.

When the doctor told you a day before the funeral
that it was actually a girl, I know it hit you harder.
The confusion. The name change. The small clothes abandoned.
Girls seem to deserve to die less.

I watched your boys play on the cemetery trees during the ceremony.
How I wanted us to join them.

I noticed
at most funerals
the only room for an audience
is among the grass and graves
seated on plastic chairs with velvet covers
upon the sloganed tombstones of the departed flights.

I wept
sitting on a man's grave with a long name—
wondered if someday
a boy would come
sit upon mine,
not wonder about the huge way I sneezed
or kissed nervously
or idea'd my way through cashless, lonely nights
inventing ways out of sorrow with pens and garage-sale lights.

And when his plastic chair rickets back
he might see my name
and notice that graves are things we walk upon
and must walk away from.

If I could un-invent shoebox sized caskets
I would do this for you.

We are mist.

JOIN THE AIRBORNE

*I thought I would die during this time in my life. It really made me glad to be
alive after that. I would like to talk to anyone thinking of joining. There is
pride for the living who make it out. And honor for the ones who don't make
it. Your Mother doesn't care about honor. And I doubt a musical will solve the
heavy inside you. Nice try.*

I asked why our foxholes needed to be so deep.
"When an enemy grenade lands in the foxhole
that you dug six feet deep, the
shrapnel will not destroy any men or equipment.
When the enemy sends a
ball of fire through your fat head,
we don't have to worry about burying your
sorry ass 'cause you've already done the work for us."
Cool.

A Drill Sergeant used to tell me
when he would be absent so the squad leaders
could beat up the 'ate up' Privates.
We beat up a guy who wet his bed before
inspection. His name was Middleton, I think. We thought we were
helping him.
We thought hurting someone would make them hard, disciplined
and focused. We were 18.

Going for weeks without even seeing a real woman
makes you want to kill even more.

A new paratrooper caught the wind into the training tower.
His chute
collapsed and he straddled the metal. Eighty feet up, he wept in pain,
waiting for the fire trucks,
hanging on for life and we joked up to him about his dead balls
'cause there was nothing else we could do.

During basic training, a friend from L.A. in my unit
tried to kill himself by
trimming his dog tags and jamming them into a light socket.
I forget his name.
Maybe Stone.

At every base is a main flagpole with a ball on top called a truk. It contains
a razor blade, a bullet and matches. It is for the commander of the base, if over-
run, to climb to the top, cut up the flag, burn it and
blow his brains out.
This darkness makes me proud.

The 82nd has a marquee near Bastogne Street. It has a number on it. If we
could make it 82 days without a training accident,
we could have a day off.
We hadn't had a day off in 10 years.

Because of the large increase in suicides near Christmas time for members of
the 82nd, the base hired a NY choreographer, Lee Yapp, a civilian, to do a musical based on making
soldiers feel good about being alive. To not off themselves. I was in it. We sang "Memory" from Cats
and "We Got a Lot of Livin' To Do" from Bye Bye Birdie. It was ridiculous. It was one
more thing we did for show.
The guy that stood next to me in one of the songs
hung himself to death. An anti-suicide show, they told us, and they chose a song from Bye Bye Birdie.

Walking through airports in beret, jump boots and secrets,
I have never felt so proud.

CHERRY

The names of the dead soldiers at the end were friends of mine, fellow soldiers who were not confirmed killed. I think terror, true terror, is born from the feeling of helplessness. This happened a few months after I got out. They tried to get me to re-up. I denied it to try and become a writer. Some of my friends stayed. I asked my friends what happened and their vision of 'The Disaster at Green Ramp' is based off their stories. 24 dead from a dumb mistake. All soldiers from my unit, the 82nd Airborne. The worst loss in peace-time since WWII. I felt like I could see it go down inside my skull and did not know why I was lucky. This poem is for Sergeant Major John Condliffe. All the way.

"C-130 rollin' down the strip
64 troopers on a one-way trip
Mission top secret, destination unknown
Don't even know if we're ever goin' home
Don't even know if we're ever goin' home"
—AIRBORNE ARMY CADENCE

I BELONG TO A PROUD AND GLORIOUS TEAM
THE AIRBORNE—THE ARMY—MY COUNTRY
I AM CHOSEN
TO SERVE THEM WELL
UNTIL THE FINAL VICTORY.
—excerpt from The U.S. Army
82nd Airborne Creed

The most memorable burger I ever had:
March 23, 1994.
Damn skippy I'll never forget the taste.

C-130s, C-141s on a training day.
The Great Gray Whales burn over the North Carolina sky,
300 paratroopers and the Pope Air Force Base.
A priest would come to pray over us before every jump,
bless the runway.
Prayers rolling out of us
like piles of unopened chutes.

He passed out 'St. Michael' necklaces to the boys:
"guardian of paratroopers."
The Father ended the blessing,
said if we prayed as much as we drank
there would be no war.
Some laughter.

St. Michael.
St. Michael is waiting for his boys.

Here on a green ramp, we would wait to chute up—
board cargo planes to dump us into unknown drop zones.
It's not just a job—it was a clever advertisement.

I VOLUNTEERED TO DO IT
KNOWING WELL THE HAZARDS OF MY CHOICE.

This adventure—strapped in like a madman,
160 pounds of gear
waiting to waddle to planes like insane penguins
in camouflage straitjacket killstuff.

I slowed down my chute inspection to pull back,
observe this unknown ceremony.
I saw what the WWII German officers called
"The Devils in Baggy Pants."

The buried fear.
The wildman face paint.
The aggressive practice jumps off the dock
into the chunk chunk wood chip pile.
The heroin puns as they chute up.

Charlie battery singing:

"The helicopter's hoverin'
it's hoverin' overhead
it's pickin' up the wounded
and droppin' off the dead
Airbooooorne shoot, shoot shoot the sonofabitch."

The unique American urgency of movement.
We had spirit.
A rigger's hands move like three-card Monte while inspecting us:

Chute on back, check.
Reserve in front, check.
Kevlar secure, check.
Weapon in place, cash.
Chemical mask on side, check.
Rucksack at knees, check.
And a nice tap toward the ammo and canteens hanging off your ass.

'You're good, Airborne.'

MY GOAL IN PEACE OR WAR IS TO SUCCEED
IN ANY MISSION OF THE DAY
OR DIE, IF NEEDS BE, IN THE TRY.

I could see how that part might slip from a recruiter's speech.

DOODLE LOO DOO DOO DO
DOODLE LOO DOO DOO DOOO

The catering truck pulled up late
playing that Dixie song that came from the horn on the General Lee
car.
Everyone rigged, on their backs, except for me.
The envy of all.

"I want to get everyone a pop, two Twinkies, some M&Ms
and a burger for dessert."
Cheers.
"But I only got 2 dollars, so fuck you guys."
Rowdy man laughter bellowed.
Smittie yelled, "You better split that shit 64 ways
or you're gonna get the bath, Cherry."

The guys with only five jumps were cherries.
Sweet way to call someone,
even someone with a ton of jumps an ate up dumbass.
The bath was a collection of filled barf bags
snuck to the man next to you

dumped on your pants one minute before the jump.
You would inevitably vomit pre- or mid-jump from the stench.
It's a beautiful indoctrination.

St. Michael is waiting for his boys.
When I got to the truck he only had one burger left.
It was so ugly and mashed
but hunger does not give a shit about beauty.

At the beginning of the runway
A C-130 and an F-16 on an approach pattern
trying to land simultaneously
mistakenly
side by side.
Sometimes an illusion,
sometimes.

The giant C-130 wing bumps the small F-16
and sends the fighter spinning
toward the earth.
An unconscious diver
limp and reeling.

I could see these two little specks
eject—eject—eject—
All the necklaces of St. Michael pressing into the loaded up and lying
paratroopers chests—
nothing to control the coming wreckage.

It came
like a meteor—
like a ball of tinfoil
you sprayed with your momma's hairspray
and lit on fire.

The raging color and demon sound of sirens melting.
A drag racer's fuel and steel spitting into the stands.

I was safe
but the men on Green Ramp could not escape
could not run

strapped down
restrained
bound by the weight of their oath
certain screaming scrambling on their backs
"Run, you sons of bitches. Run!"

With speed
you could quick release your gear in 12 seconds.
They had 10.

The way they lay there,
faces of surrender.

PFC Stephen Addington—
shotgunned Old Milwaukee beer and knew plants
Sergeant Jimenez—
drove a Camaro from upstate with no seatbelts
Private Aaron Fitzgerald—
found his wife in Korea and missed California
Staff Sergeant Jaime Interdonato—
still had 2 pinhole scars from his mother punching in his bloodwings.
Specialist Roberto Sanchez—
couldn't dance sober
Private Jeffrey Farkas—
would mute the TV and invent the words
Corporal Mike "Smittie" Smith—
the tightest hook shot since Kareem.

I stood there.
I stood.
Hands at my side,
squeezing the burger
unable to move.

The rabid, meteoric, howling metal
ghosting them one by one.
I just stood there.

All the statues of St. Michael.

CHEAP RENT

She, a strange landlord,
pointed to her chest and said,
"If you lived here
you'd be home by now."

I, the stranger with no deposit,
pointed to my chest and said,
"If you lived here
you would have to be
very—tiny."

I think of her smart hips
and the days left before their unhinging.

Our love was redder than the eyes of McCarthy.
Our love was blacklisted and strong.
Our love was a brawl in the street
with spectacles on.

Eyes of bayonet knives,
brass-knuckle sex,
crowbar quarrels
and the nunchakus of my mouth
which I tried to use with great aplomb and theatrical flash
but always ended up knocking myself unconscious.

"No, you don't look fat in that dress."
"Yes, that sentence does assume you look
fat in some dresses."

Kapow. Right in the face.

This love remains a tongue-less boy
in a basement
that you snuck graham crackers to.

He loved to see the glaze
of your hammer-and-nail polish.
You kept him alive.
He paid you with a finger every time you arrived:

One to clean your elfish ear.
Then two
to check your pulse.
Then three
to make
an unbreakable Boy Scout oath.
Then four
for sex karate.

Then five
so you could rest each one
of his loose fingers in between yours
like couples do when they stroll
through shitty carnivals.

When we first met
she told me of the brilliant in Israel
and the erotic vision of the cynic.
I tried to turn her on by talking to her about
skinning animals.
She kept hunting for a metaphor.
I was actually just talking about skinning animals.

Now I can't stop thinking of how our baby would look in a perm
with massive elk for eyebrows
and then in comes her mouth
filled with the shorebreak of Tel Aviv
on my dirty neck.

Our mouths now building a jangly, red swamp
they will call weirdo Louisiana. Jewisiana.

This kiss spills her silent résumé.

She is the poster child
for the Willy Wonka suicide camp.

Her stomach is a summer full
of black ice-cream-truck hijackings.

Her eyes are highway fatalities
you can't stop staring at.

Her skin is rehab for sandpaper junkies.

She is my landlord
and she lowers the rent,
points to her chest and says,

"Man, if you lived here
you'd be home by now."

Aquanaut

Downtown Long Beach is a woman
packed with heavy ghosts
in heavy coats
who aches when the gulls pass through her.

She is a woman changing out of her work clothes,
surrounding us in the laundry of night fog—
loosening our tourniquets with whiskey's sultry mist,
healing wounds by directing us to the warm light
of the 4th st. and Broadway dives.

Tonight, my telescope points toward her high-rise fingers,
spying the open windows for the last place God hid my ignition,
for the last place I tangled the sex in your shadow.

Tonight, there are no knives in my pocket to guard my walk.
No reason to pull the razor blade
out from behind the library card in my wallet.
No reason to soar from the green spine
of the Vincent Thomas bridge.
No reason to collapse
in the rusted regret dumpster
behind the Reno Room.

Orion awaits over Avalon.

Remember how we wanted to water ski there,
all the way to the island
on the backs of the aquarium bat-rays?

And remember how I haggled the rays into it
by giving them back their stingers?

And remember how hard you kissed me
as we mounted onto their slime and leather wings?

And remember how the rays swerved us recklessly
through the Pacific oil rig pylons?

And remember how the sensation made us feel so close to death,
it made us more alive?

We raced under wide Catalina stars, slept in a deep island sleep
until the lights over Pine Street called us home
to a tired sailboat harbor
where masts creak and sway like a brigade of crosses
marching nowhere.

You said, "Let's steal the *Queen Mary*!
We'll watch her sweep through the August glow of red tides
drinking in the tiny green fireflies of the sea."

I told you your kiss made me feel like Winston Churchill
and you said, "Powerful?"
and I said, "Drunk."

Today the Queen is at rest—still unmoved,
rusted, boilers removed, gutted and ready to live.

I spend my days looking for anchors—
plotting courses to deserted ports—
attaching more telescopes to my sailboat
in hopes that I will catch that siren,
combing her fingers through the shocks of hair
that fall from her head like thousands of wet rosaries.

If I spot you
will I see
the scars I left in your back—
mazes of amazement and black, frustrated passion?
Vanishing tattoos.

Slow halo-generator woman of Long Beach—
I will watch and wait for the look to return to your face—
the look you used to give an Aquanaut close to death,
head rocked back,
eyes pinched full of twilight and drunk fantasy. Racing away.

When the morning laughs out loud with big yellow teeth,
when the asphalt smells like a melting Buddhist,
when the sea returns what I have lost,
I will turn my telescope toward the regenerating night sky.
Orion awaits over us all.

Hot For Sorrow

*In Munich, I met the kids from a mesmerizing, brilliant group called Broken
Social Scene. I asked if they would let me use their music when I do this out
loud. They are gracious Canadians so the singer, Kevin Drew said yes.*

When the police helicopters showed up
I grabbed onto the skid
and they flew me across town
to your house.
I watched you through the glass as you slept
like jewelry in a coffin.

I screamed out

"Hey!
I don't want to be the best lover you've ever had.
I just want to be your favorite. There's a difference."

File me under hot for sorrow.

When I couldn't find your picture, I ate everyone's unwanted
videotape and dreamt.
When you appeared, soft-focused,
outlined in lasers,
embarrassed of your little T-Rex arms and seaweed hair,
we danced on the ceiling like Lionel Richie on crack
until it was time to walk you home
from naked class. A+.

This cross-eyed sniper
misses you so much.

The heavy solo night music
tells me what is buried beneath our city:

Ambulances hooked on that one ballad—
A sky turning red over its opponents.

Night melodies of helicopter switchblades
slice through this city.

The noise tells me there is still crime down here.
5000 air machines cannot stop crime.
5000 searchlights cannot stop crime.
5000 police fully moustached, with a John Wayne box-set,
and our names on every baton
cannot fully stop crime.

I now know that what I feel for you is crime.

This is why I like the sound of police choppers:
not because it makes me feel safe and watched over
but rather because it is the music of war,
and tonight
they were playing our war.

A Kick in the Chest

This page is a knife to the throat
of today's poets trying to seance the '50s Beat poets
with craftless poetry,
lame snapping fingers,
bored tongues, eyes bleeding rust all over their new berets.

I cannot be that poster.
I cannot give you what you thought you might get.
I cannot give you stoner politics.
"Rasta is neither religion nor revolution
if practiced only while baked on a couch."

I cannot be a revolution dealer
pushing for applause,
inflammatory phrases with no plan of action:
"The system, my friends, is bringin' us down, so we should fight
together now."

But how?

"How? Uh, that's not my job.
Let me finish this bong load and then we'll ask my third eye. Word
eye. Society."

Give their hearts action.
I will write until this mind becomes a roped-off crime scene
where failure was murdered.

How did the soap box turn into a broken polygraph?
This heart knows no yoga movement on the mountaintop of your
chakras. This heart is dredging gutters for other broken hearts.

This heart took an elevator to hell and brought you back text for
souvenirs. These shoulders are not to be cried upon for their blades
cut through tongues in cheeks.

The heart was once at peace but peace fit
like a tuxedo on a red light whore.
And there are whores.
Show me a poet hungry for fame and money

and I'll show you a dead actor.
I'll take a hot kiss in Hades over sex in a Mercedes.
Why?
So that if I curse the devil
my mouth can understand
the logic in the heart of the only angel denied mercy.

I want the action and the grit
and the blood inside your lips,
a knife to the throat of the poetry we knew.

It is:

A burglar breathing on your neck
stealing scenery while you sleep
and only the discarded beauty he keeps.

Like:

Hummingbirds with broken arms.
A police photo album of the suicidal breaking into heaven.
A superhero with cancer.
Boys street fighting for the feathers of dead doves.
A magazine where all the models advertise only things
that will kill you.

It's time we gave them action.
The expected is the enemy.
The plain start in the writing of that which scares you,
that which kills you.
The thing that makes you weak is the thing that makes you real.

This is for the hearts that sweat for a different kind of
muddy, scarlet, Mother I am broken
but I am still fighting kind of beauty.

Honesty is never lost in translation.

Words were our wings—
now let them be rifles.

Aim for the mess of the heart.

THE KUROSAWA CHAMPAGNE

This poem was built after watching Kurosawa's Dreams and The Lady from Shanghai by Orson Welles. It is infused with a time I watched a lover have a nightmare and did not wake her. Will-o'-the wisp is where the word wisped came from. It means a ghostly light that appears over bogs or marshes.

Tonight
your body shook,
hurling your nightmares
back to Cambodia.
Your nightgown wisped off
into Ursa Minor.

I was left here on earth feeling alone,
paranoid about the Rapture.

Tonight
I think it is safe to say we drank too much.
Must I apologize for the volume in my slobber?
Must I apologize for the best dance moves ever?
No.

Booze is my tuition to clown college.

I swung at your purse.
It was staring at me.

I asked you to sleep in the shape of a trench
so that I might know shelter.

I drew the word surrender in the mist of your breath,
waving a white sheet around your body.

In the morning, let me put on your make-up for you,
loading your gems with mascara
then I'll tell you the truth.
I watched black ropes and tears ramble down your face.

Lady war paint.
A squad of tiny men rappelled down those snaking lines
and you said,

"Thank you for releasing all those fuckers from my life."

You have a daily pill case.
There are no pills inside.
It holds the ashes of people who burned
the moment they saw you.
The cinema we built was to play the greats
but we could never afford the power
so in the dark cinema
you painted pictures of Kurosawa.

I just stared at you like Orson Welles,
getting fat off your style.

You are a movie that keeps exploding.
You are Dante's fireplace.

We were so broke,
I'd pour tap water into your mouth,
burp against your lips
so you could have champagne.

You love champagne.

Sparring in the candlelight.

Listen—
the mathematical equivalent of a woman's beauty
is directly relational to the amount or degree
other women hate her.

You, dear, are hated.

Your boots are a soundtrack to adultery.
Thank God your feet fall in the rhythm of loyalty.

If this kills me,
slice me julienne,
uncurl my veins
and fashion yourself a noose
so I can hold you
once more.

GOODNIGHT

The struggle made you fantastic.

About The Author

Derrick C. Brown is a comedian, poet and storyteller. He is the winner of the 2013 Texas Book of The Year award for Poetry. He is a former Paratrooper for the 82nd Airborne and is the president of one of what *Forbes* and *Filter Magazine* call "...one of the best independent poetry presses in the country," Write Bloody Publishing, which has launched over 115 books of poetry. He is the author of five books of poetry and three children's books. *The New York Times* calls his work, "...a rekindling of faith in the weird, hilarious, shocking, beautiful power of words."

He lives in Los Angeles.

BROWNPOETRY.COM

IF YOU LIKE DERRICK C. BROWN, DERRICK LIKES...

The Pocket Knife Bible — Anis Mojgani
Stunt Water — Buddy Wakefield
The Year of No Mistakes — Cristin O'Keefe Aptowicz
Birthday Girl with Possum — Brendan Constantine
Glitter in the Blood — Mindy Nettifee

Write Bloody Publishing distributes and promotes great books of poetry every year. We are an independent press dedicated to quality literature and book design.

Our employees are authors and artists so we call ourselves a family. Our design team comes from all over America: modern painters, photographers and rock album designers create book covers we're proud to be judged by.

We have published over 115 titles to date. We are grass-roots, D.I.Y., bootstrap believers. Pull up a good book and join the family. Support independent authors, artists and presses.

WRITEBLOODY
QUALITY AMERICAN BOOKS

**Want to know more about Write Bloody books, authors and events?
Join our maling list at**

www.writebloody.com

WRITE BLOODY BOOKS

After the Witch Hunt — Megan Falley

Aim for the Head: An Anthology of Zombie Poetry — Rob Sturma, Editor

Amulet — Jason Bayani

Any Psalm You Want — Khary Jackson

Birthday Girl with Possum — Brendan Constantine

The Bones Below — Sierra DeMulder

Born in the Year of the Butterfly Knife — Derrick C. Brown

Bring Down the Chandeliers — Tara Hardy

Ceremony for the Choking Ghost — Karen Finneyfrock

Courage: Daring Poems for Gutsy Girls — Karen Finneyfrock, Mindy Nettifee & Rachel McKibbens, Editors

Dear Future Boyfriend — Cristin O'Keefe Aptowicz

Dive: The Life and Fight of Reba Tutt — Hannah Safren

Drunks and Other Poems of Recovery — Jack McCarthy

The Elephant Engine High Dive Revival anthology

Everything Is Everything — Cristin O'Keefe Aptowicz

The Feather Room — Anis Mojgani

Gentleman Practice — Buddy Wakefield

Glitter in the Blood: A Guide to Braver Writing — Mindy Nettifee

Good Grief — Stevie Edwards

The Good Things About America — Derrick Brown & Kevin Staniec, Editors

Hot Teen Slut — Cristin O'Keefe Aptowicz

I Love Science! — Shanny Jean Maney

I Love You Is Back — Derrick C. Brown

The Importance of Being Ernest — Ernest Cline

In Search of Midnight — Mike McGee

The Incredible Sestina Anthology — Daniel Nester, Editor

Junkyard Ghost Revival anthology

Kissing Oscar Wilde — Jade Sylvan

The Last Time as We Are — Taylor Mali

Learn Then Burn — Tim Stafford & Derrick C. Brown, Editors

Have fun in Portland!
Don't run into bathroom Doors!
It's a bad time.
♡
Kelly's Couple

CPSIA information can be obtained at www.ICGtesting.com
Printed in the USA
LVOW11s1050130916

504388LV00001B/1/P